About the Author

Justin Montello has passionately taught 8th grade English for the last twelve years. He thrives on telling stories through novels, screenplays and songs. He is currently in the process of obtaining his PhD in teacher leadership, furthering a commitment to be a lifelong learner. He is a proud and dedicated father and husband. His family has set out to inspire the love of play, creating a YouTube channel called Family Fun Party. He is an inspiring leukemia survivor, hoping to influence an audience to always believe in themselves and not give up when the fight gets hard.

Grow

Justin Montello

Grow

Olympia Publishers
London

www.olympiapublishers.com
OLYMPIA PAPERBACK EDITION

Copyright © Justin Montello 2024

The right of Justin Montello to be identified as author of
this work has been asserted in accordance with sections 77 and 78 of
the Copyright, Designs and Patents Act 1988.

All Rights Reserved

No reproduction, copy or transmission of this publication
may be made without written permission.
No paragraph of this publication may be reproduced,
copied or transmitted save with the written permission of the publisher,
or in accordance with the provisions
of the Copyright Act 1956 (as amended).

Any person who commits any unauthorized act in relation to
this publication may be liable to criminal
prosecution and civil claims for damage.

A CIP catalogue record for this title is
available from the British Library.

ISBN: 978-1-80439-833-3

This is a work of fiction.
Names, characters, places and incidents originate from the writer's
imagination. Any resemblance to actual persons, living or dead, is
purely coincidental.

First Published in 2024

Olympia Publishers
Tallis House
2 Tallis Street
London
EC4Y 0AB

Printed in Great Britain

Dedication

I dedicate this book to all my previous and future students; they are the ones who continue to inspire hope in finding solutions to serious problems, impacting future generations.

Acknowledgements

I would like to thank my superhero wife, Cassie, our incredible kids, Landon, Leo and Noah, and all others who encouraged me along this journey. I would like to thank Olympia Publishers for the opportunity. Lastly, I would like to thank the people from the Cleveland Clinic for their vital care throughout the hardest time of my life.

Chapter 1

Splash! Autumn Log stomped through knee-high flood waters as lightning illuminated the night sky. Multiple fires burned simultaneously, all over the northernmost part of the Southern United States (S.U.S.).

A sign finally became visible, motivating Autumn to persevere: *New United States (N.U.S.)*. The only thing standing between her and being a fugitive—as that's what she would be upon entering the N.U.S. for *any* reason—was a watchtower with N.U.S. authority officers surveying the border that divided the two countries.

She couldn't make out what the authority officers were doing, so she dropped to the ground to get a better look. She zoomed in with her binoculars; some types of larger guns were slung over their shoulders. Four guards circled around the porch-type lookout. Sirens sang in the background, contributing to the already chaotic setting; even so, there was no movement on the authority officers' end.

Autumn figured their nonchalant attitude toward the chaos was a great indication of the current reality: People didn't care about the environment or other people anymore. Her father, Barto, would always say things like *It's as if we set a new "world record" for the hottest day on Earth every single day.* That, along with the sporadic, unpredictable weather—heat waves and such, causing uncontrollable fires, floods and dangerous winds, was all the more reason for Autumn to carry out her family's plan. Their plan was to save the planet by using their recently discovered super power: regrowing trees once they'd been chopped down. This was a big deal, as many countries either outlawed, or at least closely limited the number of trees it allowed, thanks to their benefits being lost in translation over the years.

Society seemed to accept the common occurrence of unpredictable, weather-stricken emergencies being part of everyday life. This allowed authority officers to focus on what they perceived to be greater tasks at hand. Regardless of the country, leaders seemed to prioritize keeping people within their specific borders—there were now seven new countries derived from the former United States of America. Besides that, leaders also shared commonalities when it came to establishing and maintaining power; they tried to control everyone's moves.

However, Autumn was prepared; she had a plan; she just needed to create a distraction that would send the authority officers running. She felt a rumble; it was an aftershock, a result of a recent earthquake that caused the ground to shake. It was her chance; she scoured the dirty ground, searching for the stump of where a tree once stood. The darkness of the sky made it a bit more challenging than originally anticipated. The good news is that the Log family never let a challenge deter them.

She finally found the stump. She checked her materials list one more time. She had all the necessary items in place. She removed her tarp from her backpack, covered the materials as they rested on top of the stump, and removed it. The moon and stars must've conferenced, because a ray of light looked like it connected them in a dot-like manner, momentarily illuminating the night sky. A ten-foot-high tree shot up from the stump, fully leafed.

Autumn, now used to this tree-regrowing phenomenon,

raced away from the scene, out of the way of flying debris. Again, she adjusted her binoculars and checked on the authority officers. The light in the sky *did* make them take notice. The tree was so out of place, that it grabbed their attention. They sounded an alarm—a different one, further contributing to the chaotic setting. Autumn used the intended distraction to her advantage, and she snuck into the N.U.S. Her plan worked. Autumn Log, now *fugitive*, completed phase one of her family's plan: she regrew another tree and snuck into the N.U.S.

Chapter 2

"Leo, honey, wake up!"

"I'm up, Mom!" Leo grunted, his head still on his pillow.

"You don't want to be late for school!" she hollered.

He got up and threw on a pair of jeans and a t-shirt. He walked down the stairs, into the kitchen where the rest of his family was getting ready for their day.

"Where's your coat?" Ashton, Leo's dad, was bothered.

"It's seventy-five degrees today. Ohio isn't like it was in the ancient days. We technically fall into a tropical environment," responded Lucy, who defended her older brother. Leo smiled, appreciative of the support, especially since Lucy was the genius of the family.

"Can you guys drop me off a little earlier today?" asked Lewis. He always caught rides with his older brother and sister on their way to high school. Lewis was in middle school and looked up to his siblings.

"No problem," Leo assured. "We have to get moving though. I told Mr. Holt that I'd come in early today. We're starting a lesson about trees."

"What? Why are you wasting time learning about trees?" Ashton asked.

"Learning isn't a waste of time," his mom, Rosie, protested.

"I'm just saying, every house has one tree on their property. That's that. There's nothing to learn. We use them for materials," fired Ashton.

As the Oliver kids made their way to their car, Ashton and Rosie continued bickering. "What are you doing encouraging this new, now never-ending interest in trees?"

"I think critical thinking is a good thing, Ashton," Rosie never backed down from confrontation.

"You know if they ask too many questions—or knowing our kids, spark ideas for change—they could be in grave danger." Although it was only them in the house, Ashton still whispered out of habit, "President Jamen could have us all *killed*."

Rosie nodded, knowing he was right. The only problem: Both she and Ashton were open to challenging the government themselves. The difference: They knew how to balance government jobs while fully controlling their actions and beliefs; teenagers sometimes lack that control.

Leo dropped off his sister at the doors of Maplewood High School, drove around Veteran's Stadium—the obsolete football field, and dropped off Lewis at Jaguar Middle School. Leo drove back to the high school, parked his car, opened his door, and kept singing the words of L.L.4.Cool.K's latest hit, "Shake Your Butt-Butt But Don't Break My Button" – the best song on the NOW 1,444 CD.

Upon entering school, he was searched as usual. Small-town security guards patrolled the entrance to prevent students from bringing weapons into the building. In addition, security guards often monitored students during testing time, to make sure they didn't cheat. They were pretty cool for the most part; most security guards were former Maplewood athletes who could have gone professional. Unfortunately, sports didn't have professional teams anymore.

"What's up, my man!" one of the security guards who graduated just a few years ago knew Leo pretty well.

"What's going on?" Leo opened his backpack, familiar with the drill at this point. Once nothing illegal was found, he entered. "Still lifting?"

"Five years, man!" the security guard was alluding to the major controversy regarding athlete pay just five years prior. Sports in the N.U.S. were cancelled, President Jamen's orders. Otherwise, this security guard would probably be playing professional football.

"If you meatheads would've accepted the hundred million dollar league minimum, we wouldn't be in this problem," Leo half-heartedly joked.

"Man," the security guard elongated the pronunciation of the word while lightly mean-mugging Leo. "Listen, we were the country's main source of entertainment. Everyone else in this country is so money-hungry and selfish; how do you want us not to be? Now my fellow athletes and I are stuck policing you little…"

"Later, boss!" Leo left the conversation good-naturedly.

Leo headed to Mr. Holt's classroom. He helped him prepare lessons some days, shutting down ideas that he knew classmates would dislike. "Let's do something hands-on today," he suggested.

"Absolutely," Mr. Holt concurred. "I have just the thing. We're going to act out the importance of trees. We will also do a creative writing piece inviting students to envision what would happen if we had no trees at all."

"Sounds fun," Leo agreed. "Actually, intriguing. Why does each tree lawn have just one tree?"

Ding! The bell let everyone know it was time for first period.

"Ah!" Mr. Holt started, "Hold that thought!"

Students filed into class with morning eyes, annoyed by Mr. Holt's cheerful attitude. "Good morning, everyone! Welcome to

October 10th, 2199. Welcome to the best day yet. Today, we have a great lesson. As we know, ever since the country's split nearly one hundred years ago, the government has monitored trees. *Why*? I ask you. Were they important hundreds, thousands of years ago? They must be good for something besides making money from material goods. No? What policies are the six other countries—that once made the former United States of America—abiding by regarding the environment? Why are we not privy to that information?"

The students' ears were glued to Mr. Holt, as the approaching forty year old with slightly gray hair sparked interest. Students respected Mr. Holt, mostly because he respected them. He challenged teenagers to share their thoughts; he listened; it was clear he cared about the youth. This was out of the ordinary in the N.U.S., especially in the educational field.

Mr. Holt went on to explain how thousands of years ago people thought trees were needed for humans and animals to breathe. That without trees, life as we knew it wouldn't be possible on planet Earth. They were oxygen, homes, medicines and protection. He then made connections to the ever-changing, unpredictable weather that *is* Ohio. Finally, he encouraged students to write about the good pertaining to trees, keeping these ideas in perspective. "Four minutes on the clock. Writers, write!"

Beep! When the timer expired, Sarah, the most stylish girl in school, stood up and read her poem: "Trees, trees, helped people cure diseases. They're good cuz' they help block the sun, why does President Jamen allow us only 1? ☺ "

The class was impressed with Sarah's rhymes. They snapped their fingers in unison, per classroom tradition when somebody shared a piece of writing. Mr. Holt was right; he did have the perfect lesson. He planted a new interest, a new love, an infatuation of trees in Leo and his classmates' heads.

Chapter 3

For lunch, Leo headed to the local fast-food place for a quick bite. He parked his car and walked through the drive-thru like he'd done so many times before.

"Welcome to BigLand Burgers. Please begin your order in 5, 4, 3, 2, 1, go," a robot's voice spoke.

"I'll have two burgers, two United fries and two bottled waters, please," Mr. Holt shouted from behind. "I'll get your lunch today." Mr. Holt loved him some BigLand Burgers. They walked around the window and watched the machine make their food. It was a big deal for people to watch how their food was prepared. Not only was it a source of entertainment, but it was a peace of mind as well. There had been rumors of the government poisoning peoples' food, and now all restaurants had to allow people to watch their food as it was being made.

"How long has the world been this way?"

"What do you mean?" asked Mr. Holt.

"Well, I mean, years and years ago did they have machines cooking United fries in front of everyone?"

"Many people believe different things." Mr. Holt began to whisper, "At one time, United fries were called French fries. The New United States used to be connected from California to Maine to Florida. We used to trade and be allies with other countries beyond the former United States. I suppose there were a million small disturbances and nobody could get along, and that's why we're no longer connected. But at one time, I'd like to believe people cooked for other people and there were many jobs because of food."

"So, at one time, restaurants provided jobs for *people*?" Leo inquired, already knowing the answer.

"Yes. Now it seems everyone works in some form of security; that way the country is able to keep tabs on everyone at all times. Being searched at school and having cameras in every classroom, on every street corner, was not the norm. That machine that is cooking our food is watching us as well," Mr. Holt raised his eyebrows and looked at Leo.

"$179.56 please," said that same robot voice.

"We're not as advanced as some people thought we'd be. People thought we'd have flying cars; we don't. Machines just took the place of people in many cases. Trees used to be seen as beautiful and beneficial; now we only see them as a business opportunity to create materials and overcharge folks for them. We don't have many left, but I think we need them. That's why I think there's one per tree lawn," Mr. Holt slid his money through a slot that you might see at an arcade token exchange.

"I have a feeling, Mr. Holt, that trees have something to do with us. Something huge," Leo stared up at the sky. "If I tell you a secret, can you keep it?"

Mr. Holt was worried. He stuttered, "I-I mean, umm, I can do my best, but if it's—" he was cut off.

"There are thirty-three trees in my backyard. It's the only place I—or my family—have ever seen one besides the tree lawns."

"*Really?*" Mr. Holt's tone changed dramatically. One could sense the fear permeating from his body language. "Who else knows?"

"Don't be afraid for me. I'm not going to do anything stupid.

I know my place."

"Ya know, Leo, the government has been doing a decent job protecting us and giving us some freedoms," Mr. Holt tried to diffuse the situation. "Maybe we should just focus on what the next big thing is, as opposed to being concerned about the past." Mr. Holt looked at Leo, knowing it was no use reasoning with a teenager.

"I'll let you know what I find out," Leo insinuated an investigation into the trees in his backyard was inevitable.

Chapter 4

Later that evening, Lewis and Leo were playing catch in the backyard.

"How old do you guys think this house is? Just take a guess." Leo asked his siblings, as Lucy was nearby working on finalizing her United Language paper.

"Mom and Dad made some updates, but I'd say at least one hundred years old," Lucy calculated.

The home had a black and grayish tone, but it also had a vibrant, feel-good vibe; the colors gave the house a unique feel. It was very inviting, but at the same time, mysterious. The backyard was huge. Part of the yard was surrounded by an old reddish, rusting fence. Sometimes when Lewis threw his curveball, it'd miraculously find its way to the fence, as if the ball and fence were magnets. Leo would stare through the steel, peek through the iron octagons and scan for any cameras monitoring the area. The kids knew to never, under any circumstance, hop that fence. They figured cameras were in places they couldn't see.

"Thirty-three of them," Leo invited his siblings to join in on the curiosity.

"We have this house for a *reason*," Lewis, the sure-minded middle schooler proclaimed.

Lucy, being the more logical sibling, noted, "Our house *is* the only property that has a view of them. It *does* seem rather unmaintained... abandoned. There might be a reason."

"I wonder what other countries' laws are?" questioned Leo, hoping Lucy had some insider-genius scoop, unknown to anyone else.

"Each nation operates as independently as possible. Traveling from country to country is forbidden because of hostility toward one another. Most governments use fear to control their people," Lucy speculated. "At least that's what I've found in my independent research on the dark web."

Leo grabbed the ball and tossed it back to Lewis. "Snap your wrist earlier next time, B," B was a nickname, short for brother, that the Oliver boys adopted. "Gosh!" Lewis did *not* snap his wrist earlier. The ball raced back to the fence. On the way up from picking up the baseball, something caught Leo's eye. He did a double-take. There was a ray of light that flickered on-again, off-again as if someone had a flashlight. "Hey—" It vanished.

"Come on!" Lewis moaned.

Leo hustled back to the house, officially creeped out.

Chapter 5

The next morning, Ally—the Oliver's family cat—woke up Leo with her purrs. She lay atop of his chest, an unwelcome alarm clock.

"Oh, Ally, I couldn't sleep at all," he covered his face with a pillow.

"B, we're running late," Lewis flung the bedroom door open.

"Yo, I think I'm staying home today. I feel like crap."

"Mom!" Lewis yelled. "Leo is faking being sick… again!"

Rosie made her way into the bedroom to investigate. She spoke without even needing words; her looks were suspicious enough to prompt a rebuttal from Leo.

"Mom, I don't feel right. I think it was the sloppy joes. Plus, I couldn't sleep a wink."

"This *has* to be the last time!" she demanded and walked away.

"It will be. I promise. I love school…" Leo tried to sound convincing. He still earned a patented eye roll from Lewis. Leo simply shrugged, accepting the win.

It wasn't long before Ashton was out the door; he worked for a government legal consultant firm. Rosie had to hustle to do a school drop off and make it to work on time; she worked at a fancy thirty-five-story high-rise that specialized in organizing various areas of government data.

"Well, Ally, I guess it's just us today," Leo picked up his binoculars—a gift from his grandfather. They were admittedly dusty from lack of use. "Hope Florida is going well, Papa," he said aloud as if Ally understood him. He'd never met him since there was a travel ban between countries, but he'd heard enough stories to feel as if he did know his grandfather.

He peered out his window which overlooked the area. "There's way more space back there. It's probably two football fields long." Leo zigzagged with the binoculars, investigating closer than ever before. Hours ticked by. No sign of any: movement, authority officers, vehicles, or cameras… a forgotten area. Leo was baffled. "What the heck?" defeat started to settle in. As he was exhaling, he noticed the inscription on the binoculars: *Can't give up now.* Leo always looked for signs to help guide the way. He decided to continue to watch the property but this time from a different angle. He went downstairs, to the back porch, to get a more ground-level view. "What the?" Pieces of dirt jumped up from the ground. Someone—or something—was causing it to happen. He adjusted his binoculars. Someone was on their property, shoveling a hole in the Oliver's backyard. Leo's heart sprinted, suddenly stunned.

Chapter 6

There was no reasonable explanation that someone would be in his backyard. His family was out; his neighbors lived too far away to have any idea as to where the property line was drawn.

The hooded figure stood up and stretched. Leo's back hugged the wall, out of view. He could only seem to breathe heavily; his mind seemed to rise above his body; adrenaline was building. He snuck back up to his bedroom to grab a large memorabilia item that hung on his wall: a Cleveland Captains wooden baseball bat. The Captains were the town's baseball team before sports were banned. The fight-or-flight response clicked to fight. This hooded person was in trouble. Leo stood six feet, two inches tall and weighed a buck-eighty.

Leo tiptoed around the corner of the house. He developed a visual line. He analyzed the bat, and took deep breaths, trying to conceive the courage to attack. He was about to turn the corner and rush, swinging and screaming, but he was interrupted by a whistle. The person was whistling a familiar tune, even though Leo couldn't quite put his finger on it. It bewildered him because this person was comfortable enough to whistle while working on his family's property. They had been there before. Terror now resided in his mind.

It was go time. He raced from behind the brick, screaming. The person turned around as he was mid-swing. Leo's eyes widened; he realized it was a girl, but his momentum carried out the follow-through of the swing: *Whack! Plop!* Autumn Log fell like a tree being chopped to the ground, knocked out.

Chapter 7

The bat connected with her back. That was the first time he had hit someone or been in a fight of any sort. He naively checked her pulse, uncertain what to do. He pulled her inside the house—a tougher task than you'd think. He was able to lift her onto the family's brown, faux-leather couch. He fetched her a glass of ice water and sat in his father's rocking chair, waiting for her to wake up. His nerves eased a bit; it helped that Autumn was the most beautiful girl he'd ever seen. Plus, he kept the baseball bat in hand.

As the ice in that water was starting to melt, Ally casually made her way down the stairs into the family room. She jumped onto the couch and onto Autumn's chest. Leo couldn't stop it; his body was in limbo trying to react. It was too late, Autumn shot up, catapulting Ally.

"Where am I?" she shouted.

Ally made a gymnast-like landing and scooted off into hiding.

Leo held out his hands and pushed them down in an effort to ease worries. "You're inside my house. You are safe. But I do have some questions for you."

"I'm so sorry!"

"What are you doing on my family's property?"

"Wow, is this water safe to drink?"

"Safe?"

"Where I'm from, clean drinking water is a hot commodity."

"Where are you from? What are you doing here?"

"I was researching the area with the thirty-three trees, Leo."

"Who are you?" he grew more uneasy by the second. "How do you know my name?"

"I'm Autumn Log. I'm from the S.U.S. and I have been spying on your family this past week."

"Hmm," Leo shot a confused, passive-aggressive look. Then he looked at the bat again, raising his eyebrows to Autumn as if to suggest he was thinking of using it again.

"Easy, slugger," she joked to diffuse the situation. "I can explain."

"Please."

She inhaled deeply, "Years ago, trees helped the planet very much. As time went on, greed settled in, resulting in a need for this natural resource. Trees could do so much good: protect the planet from the sun, help us breathe, serve as homes for countless species, and fight against pollution. I know ya'll have one per tree lawn, but that is not nearly enough."

Leo cut in quickly, "I am with you; we have been learning about this at school."

"Your teachers better be careful. I can't imagine the government wants that happening."

The idea of something bad happening to Mr. Holt started to marinate in Leo's mind.

Autumn went on, "We have so little left that over the next few months—by New Year's Day, I have reason to believe a pattern of extreme weather will destroy the entire Eastern Seaboard of the former United States. I'm from the S.U.S., Florida specifically. Our land will be submerged, spontaneously, and continuous natural disasters will turn the country into a whirlwind of turmoil. People will start to die. Fires, floods, wind storms, you name it. Other countries overseas have been experiencing this for decades. Every aspect of life on this planet is endangered."

"Why should I believe this is true? You are a convict after all."

"Come on! It hasn't snowed in Ohio in years. You know something more serious is bound to happen if we don't make change."

"What can we do if the government is in charge? We can't make change."

"Well, my family *is* doing something. We refuse to sit by while the hottest temperatures on record still continue to climb. The rising ocean levels, floods and fires are destroying land, homes, and taking lives. I fled here to help regrow trees in this area and to fight against these threats. But I literally fled during one of the worst storms in Florida's history. When I left, over fifty people died due to the storm."

Leo thought of his grandfather. "I have family in Florida."

"What part?"

"I wouldn't know if you said it. I have no idea what Florida even looks like on a map."

Autumn reached into her hoodie pocket, "I know maps are prohibited," she pulled out a folded piece of paper, "but here is what the war-torn former United States currently looks like."

Leo analyzed the map closely. "Why would people allow these to basically go extinct?"

"Money. People don't care about anything but *it*. Trees are great natural resources; people remade them into materialistic goods," Autumn said with her southern accent. Leo was looking at her with a smug smile. "What?"

"Nothing. It's just even television shows from the S.U.S. are illegal. I've never heard anyone with your accent before."

"Please don't be mad at me for breaking onto your property."

"Were you going to dig a tunnel to the area?" Leo was now standing and walking around.

"Why were you and Lewis going to?" Autumn rose to her feet.

"Okay, stop."

"Stop what?"

"Stop talking about my family! It's messed up that you have been spying on us. You're a fugitive. Why shouldn't I call the authorities?" Leo's mind was a mosh pit.

"I haven't been watching your family. I have been intrigued by them and accidentally heard you all talking as I was watching the area." A few seconds of silence flooded the room. Autumn continued, "You have a great family," she smiled. "I know so much about the area. I can help you guys."

"And how do you know so much about the area?"

"My great-great-great-great grandfather, Dr. Rea Log had an extraordinary idea. I can tell you about it if you'd like." Leo's nod encouraged her to continue. "My family's story starts like this…"

*

First Flashback
"Wake up, Rea," Maggie nudged.

"Mom, what is it?" Rea rolled onto his side, wiping his goopy eyes.

"Your father and I have been up all night making you something."

Rea didn't say anything. He sparked up and shot downstairs.

His bare feet hit the cool, wood floors, as he sprinted to his soon-to-be office. He pushed open the French doors and walked inside.

"What do you think, son?" Nicko asked him in a raspy voice. "Took us both all night, haven't been to bed yet."

"I love it! The bookshelf, the chair, the curtains!"

"From our store," Nicko chimed in, proud of his small drapery business.

Rea continued, "And the desk. The desk is amazing," he ran his hand over the smooth wood.

"Your father chopped down a tree in the backyard to make that."

"It's perfect," Rea smiled.

"Now Maplewood's pride can do all of the research he wants," Nicko encouraged.

"I labeled a file for this year's findings. It has *2014* on the top," Maggie said.

"Thank you both so much," Rea expressed his gratitude.

Rea Log was everyone's top pick to change the world. When teachers couldn't make it into school, he taught the class that day. He was fourteen years old and enrolled in every advanced or college prep course. He was infatuated with the state of the environment. His favorite teacher, Mike Etre, often challenged him to find ways to conserve trees. Together, they shared data and conducted experiments. Three years of this went by, which resulted in Rea having his pick of the top colleges and universities in the United States.

However, due to Rea's extraordinary talents, he elected to skip college. Instead, he stayed home to continue his studies. He convinced Maggie and Nicko to support him financially until he was twenty-three years old. Maggie practiced what Rea preached daily… mostly about the conservation of energy.

"Why can't everyone just reuse bags when they go to the store?" she'd say, as she'd check out at the local Small Dove supermarket. "Or just carpool? Or not use lights when it's daytime?" Maggie would open her drapes in her bedroom when she needed to brush her teeth during the day; she only let the water run at the end of her brushings, to briefly rinse her spit down the sink; this was significant as she brushed her teeth *seven* times per day.

Nicko carpooled to the drapery and mapped out his stops on the way home to make sure he was as environmentally conscious as possible. Nicko would plant a tree after he did any job at a hospital or retirement home, as trees were proven to reduce stress and speed up the healing process.

Rea and Mike Etre had the Maplewood science students do experiments all year long. They were very close to developing an environmental savior: trees that could be regrown once already used. The idea seemed crazy, but after all, so does fighting, and people do that all the time for some reason.

Rea was hard at work in his office, testing different types of tree bark, when he heard Maggie call for him. "Rea! Quick!"

Rea flew from his chair into the living room. Nicko was on the floor, not moving. "I'll carry him. Start the car."

Maggie raced toward the garage. Rea lifted his father in his arms. He carried him to the hybrid van—the same one Rea adjusted so it'd get two hundred miles per gallon—and buckled him in the front seat.

Boom! Maggie sent the van in reverse, creating a van-shaped hole in the garage.

"Mom!"

"Don't tell me how to drive!" she barked back.

Even at twenty-three, Rea still knew when and when not to

talk back to his mother. Maggie got Nicko to the hospital just as two paramedics were walking inside. They grabbed a stretcher and wheeled him to the emergency room. Rea pried Maggie's hands off the stretcher, and they waited for a doctor to come tell them some news.

"Mrs. Log?" a doctor stepped into the waiting area about a half hour later.

"Yes."

"I'm Dr. Salt. It's nice to meet you. Your husband is going to be just fine. He has a mild concussion."

"What?" Rea asked.

"Yeah, he's back there rambling on about how he fell off a ladder at work today while he was trying to hang some curtains. Since he did not take care of himself right away, the symptoms worsened."

"I had no idea," Maggie said.

"He'll be just fine. Interestingly enough, he did say something about his son developing ideas to help the environment. Is that you?"

"Yes, I'm Rea Log."

"Pleasure," they shook hands. "You both can go see Nicko now, but let's chat when you're done."

After checking on his father, Rea did just that. "Dr. Salt, I believe that trees play a humongous factor in stopping the vast changes in climate, unpredictable and harmful weather patterns, and for supplying both animals and humans with oxygen."

Dr. Salt added, "Don't forget protection from the sun."

"Right, and the melting of glaciers and ice caps may lead to land loss."

"Not good for a planet that has a population higher than ever before."

"Exactly," Rea connected with Dr. Salt. "My colleague, Mike Etre, and I have many experiments in progress."

"Why don't you head up the new Environmental Department here at the hospital?"

"Really?"

"Yes, you sound like a perfect candidate. It focuses on finding beneficial things in nature to promote health in humans and animals. And of course, you can still do your experiments because trees are directly related to the well-being of, well, *beings*," Dr. Salt smiled.

When Rea and Maggie took Nicko home, he was filled with positive energy. "I'm so proud of you, my son!"

"We both are," Maggie smiled.

"When do you start?" Nicko hollered.

"Tomorrow," Rea answered.

"Perfect! There's no time like *now* to change the world!" Nicko shouted. He pointed to a watch that he always wore. It was black and white. The watch didn't have traditional numbers spread out on its face; instead, the word *Now* sporadically took up the digits' usual space. "The time is always now."

Rea packed up his black four-door hybrid and drove to his first day of work at his new job. He was stunned that after his ten-minute commute to the hospital, he came across his own parking spot. He was excited, nervous, and giddy; he felt like he had to pee and was a little shaky. After a few deep breaths, he wrapped his work bag around his shoulder, and confidently walked through the electric sliding doors and into his new place of employment.

The elevator lifted passengers up like a magic carpet to the twelfth floor. *Bing,* the all-glass elevator let the passengers out. Rea looked up and walked through a busy, yet silent research facility.

"Rea? Welcome. Hello, my name is Summer. I am a nurse at the hospital and a volunteer in the research center," were the words said quickly by a stunningly beautiful woman wearing glasses.

"Wow. A volunteer and a nurse, huh?" Rea managed to appear more impressed than amazed.

"Yes. I don't own a television and I have no life," Summer joked sarcastically.

Rea was speechless as a five foot, six inch, curly, brown-haired beauty with green eyes stood before him. She wore glasses that climbed her nose just a little bit as she smiled and flashed her perfect, pearly whites. Her bluish-blackish-polka-dot blouse and her dark, tan pencil skirt, accompanied by black shoes with a mini heel, had Rea drooling.

Summer and Rea spent many *long, long, long* hours together conducting all sorts of experiments. October 28th, 2014 was an important date for the two. It was the first time they had the best java truck around, *Cassie's Coffee Stand,* outside of work. They enjoyed each other's company so much that Rea invited her to Sunday family dinners, along with Mike Etre and Dr. Salt. The six of them always talked about trees and the environment. They were a team. A team that grew closer as years passed.

Eventually, Rea proposed to Summer using his great-great-grandmother's wedding ring. He popped the question by having Summer read a *Congrats on Your Engagement* card. She was stunned to turn around and see him on one knee. The orange sunset and the view from the back porch were beautiful. The new house they bought in Maplewood, Ohio turned into a home. A home that embodied trees and greens that went on forever. A wetland was home to cranes, ducks, geese, and other forms of countless wildlife.

"This is the perfect place to experiment," Summer noted.

"We can work on health effects at work and planet effects at home," Rea smiled.

So continued the experiments. Mike Etre had students working at school. Rea and Summer made what they called *Recycled Trees*. They chopped down a tree and surrounded the stump with a large plastic tube. Then, they placed all the chopped wood from that tree inside of the tube, allowing the materials to lay upon one another. They hoped it might spark a regrowing process by reassembling itself naturally.

Chapter 8

"Well… that's the beginning of my family's story," Autumn awaited Leo's response.

"So, this connects back to your comment about regrowing trees."

"Yes, I can fill you in more."

"Listen, I am going to help you. I just need to get my family on board if we have any real chance at this working. Do you feel comfortable communicating your rationale and family's story to my family?"

"I would feel comfortable doing that, but I can't put them at risk. That's what you're signing you and your family up for by helping me."

"Is it just exploring the area? Did Rea and Summer build my house?" Leo was piecing the puzzle together.

"That's correct. That's how and why I am connected to the area. Maybe you can help me with my initial plan to explore the area, and based on our findings, we can see if you want to involve your family." Autumn's concern helped Leo to trust her more.

"What's the plan?" Leo got up to get a drink. "Do you want something to eat or drink?"

"I'm still good with the water, thanks," Autumn appreciated the polite manners, conversation, and she didn't mind his good looks either. "I am nearly finished with a tunnel that leads from your property to a shed in the area that might house some important documents."

"A tunnel?"

"Yes, I used the chunk of grass to cover the entrance. I should be ready for a covert mission tomorrow night."

"I'll inform my brother and sister; they'll want to help. Lucy is wicked smart and Lewis is fearless. We can meet you outside around eleven p.m. My parents are usually asleep by then."

"Sounds good," Autumn concurred. Then an awkward silence filled the air. The plan was set. Neither knew what to do next. "I suppose I'll go back to digging now."

"I'll come to help," Leo offered.

"No, it's ok. I'm almost done. Plus, your family will be home soon. Think about how you'll persuade your siblings to help." With that, Autumn looked to exit the house. She tried one door that led to a closet.

Leo chuckled, "Here, it's this way. I'll get the door for you."

"No, you don't have to," Autumn reached for the doorknob at the same time. Their two touched hands.

"So sorry," Leo fumbled.

"It was my fault," Autumn hustled outside as fast as she could. The awkwardness was painful, and they both could feel it. The good news: they both felt a spark.

Chapter 9

The night carried on as usual. At the dinner table, Leo didn't say much. He knew he was up to no good and didn't want his parents to find out. He didn't want to act weird and have them question him. Unfortunately, despite his best efforts, he was acting more eccentric than ever.

"Can you please pass the *sweet* potatoes?" Leo's voice cracked as he said sweet.

Lucy just looked down at her plate, almost embarrassed for him. Lewis gave him a glance as if to say, *what are you hiding?* Internally, it was the most exhausting meal, but they made it through.

After dinner, Rosie and Ashton relaxed in the living room. It was the perfect opportunity for the kids to sneak into the basement and make music. Their parents believed them, too, because that's usually what they did in their spare time.

"You'll never believe what happened today."

"What?" Lewis knew it had to be good.

"So, I was watching the area and saw somebody in our grass. I snuck around and hit them with a baseball bat. It turns out she's a girl from the S.U.S.," Leo ripped off the band-aid.

"Are you serious?" Lucy couldn't believe it.

"She claims that the trees over in the area are important. That if we don't create more, the world will end within the next few months. We need to help her in whatever way we can; I am not sure what that looks like yet. However, if nothing changes by the

New Year, extreme weather is going to be constant, costing lives."

Lewis was skeptical, "Super sus, B!"

"I thought so, too. But you should have seen the look in her eyes," Leo shot back.

"When does she need our help?" asked Lucy.

"Tomorrow night."

"Does she just live outside?" Lewis was still super sus.

"I guess," Leo admitted. "I snuck her down some leftovers. I was thinking of putting it outside the door." Their basement had an entrance and was a great living space for the kids.

"Okay, well I guess we'll meet her tomorrow night and brainstorm the plan," Lucy headed upstairs.

"Hope she doesn't murder us," Lewis followed.

"She won't!" Leo confirmed. He decided to stay downstairs. He'd always use writing as a tool to calm his mind. He wrote in verses. He and Lewis would add instrumentals and create music; *hitting the studio* is what they called it. Leo wasn't really good when it came to talking about his feelings. But, if he made a beat, he could write it down and express himself without anyone judging him. Lewis was the only one who ever heard them. They'd written roughly 400 songs. He tapped out a beat on his drum machine, nodded his head, forgot about the world and wrote lyrics.

Confused
To say the least
Do I beast?
Save these trees
And then leave?
After all, Autumn got everything I need
I could see—us grow

I could see us glow

Then all of a sudden, he heard a *cahlink*. Little wood chips sprinkled the door frame. Leo hesitantly approached, happy to see Autumn standing there, looking over her shoulder. Their smiles mirrored their feelings: genuine happiness to see one another. Leo let Autumn inside.

"Here, I brought you some leftovers," he handed her a to-go container that contained a sweet potato and some pizza rolls. "It's nothing special, but I figured you'd be hungry."

"Thank you!" She was impressed by his kindness but more taken back by the subtle hand graze they shared. They immediately made eye contact and looked away even faster. Leo smiled and took a few steps back.

"I didn't know if I'd see you outside tonight," he started. Neither knew how to approach the situation. Besides a few homecoming dates, which were mostly with friends, neither had been on a real date before. Here they were: alone in Leo's basement, the perfect scenario, only if they weren't still strangers. "I was going to come looking for you." Leo spun around and found some blankets and pillows. "And, here. Why don't you sleep on the couch in the basement? There's a bathroom; my parents will never know." Autumn seemed different from most girls he knew in Maplewood. She was confident, smart, and trying to help people… the right amount of danger.

"Oh, that's okay," Autumn said. "I just finished the tunnel and saw you through the doors. I just wanted to let you know we're ready to go anytime tomorrow. I didn't want to be a burden."

"Not at all," Leo darted a response. "In fact, I have to insist you stay. You're a mess," he smiled.

"Is that how you get all the girls? With lines like that?" she sarcastically and accidentally flirted.

"Something like that. Listen, I'll be upstairs if you need anything," he turned and waved.

"Good night," Autumn wasn't sure if she wanted him to leave.

"Oh, one more thing: feel free to shower and eat when you hear us leave for school in the morning. We can plan tomorrow when we get home; we'll sneak our way onto the area after sunset." They were in sync.

Chapter 10

Beep! Beep! Beep! Leo's alarm let him know it was six a.m. He set it extra early in an effort to help Autumn sneak out of the basement. He was interrupted mid wake-up by the sound of footsteps coming from downstairs. One thousand bricks fell from his throat to his stomach. He tiptoed as fast as he could to see who it was. When he got to the kitchen, nobody was there. All of a sudden, the basement door shot open.

"Good morning," Ashton arrived with some dishwashing soap; they kept the extra in the basement storage.

"Good morning, Dad," Leo managed. "Couldn't wait to do the dishes, eh?"

"Best part of my day," Ashton was still a tad zombie-like this early in the morning. "What are you doing up so early?"

"I was going to get my notebook… I was studying late last night…" he went toward the stairs.

"I know. That's good. But you forgot to lock the sliding door," Ashton informed.

Leo's eyes widened, concerned how much he knew. "Oh, no."

"It's okay. There are enough cameras around the city that if anyone ever broke in, we'd catch them. But we have to be better about being safe."

"I agree. Sorry. It won't happen again," he darted down the stairs. No evidence of Autumn… or anyone. The couch looked unused. The leftover container was gone. The shower was dry.

He laid back on the couch and exhaled for what felt like the first time that morning.

The Oliver kids finished getting ready for school. Leo peered at the area as they got in the car, looking for Autumn. No trace. On the way, they jammed out to L.L.4.COOL.K.'s, "Shake Your Butt-Butt But Don't Break A Button." It was fire.

Lewis and Lucy seemed to be acting normal amidst the situation. That wasn't the case for Leo; he had sweaty palms, his heart raced, and his movement was nearly robot-like. He looked around the school building, noticing the vast number of cameras watching everyone. He often wondered who was doing the watching. Rumors flew around the school that the government was even watching, not just the principals. Sometimes he'd get lost inside his head, thinking the worst. He beelined to Mr. Holt's classroom.

"Good morning!" Leo announced.

"Happy Friday!"

"More lessons on trees?"

Mr. Holt looked around the corner, "Yes, but let's keep it down, please. I can get in trouble for teaching this stuff."

"Why? It's the truth."

"Unfortunately, some people—even those in powerful positions—choose to ignore the truth for personal gain. They're more afraid of losing power or changing than they are of fictitious things like zombies and vampires."

"Perception is reality, as you always say," Leo was still disappointed.

After Mr. Holt's class, the day went on as usual: students sat at desks and tuned in to whatever the teacher lectured for that day.

During lunch, Leo sat down to eat with some friends. One of

those friends, Savannah, kept talking about trees. "Trees are so wild to me. Why are they so special? Mr. Holt makes it seem like they were so helpful at one point."

"We still have some," Sierra, another friend, commented.

"They absorb carbon dioxide; that helps with the temperatures here," Cole—Leo's best friend, contributed to the conversation, and his passion started to bleed through. "Plus, they remove air pollution so we can breathe better."

Leo chimed in, "Drinking water is safer when we have more trees as well… according to Mr. Holt."

Savannah didn't need another second to think about it, "We should plant more."

"Shh!" Leo and Cole shushed simultaneously. They looked around to make sure nobody heard them.

"What's the big deal?" Sierra questioned.

"Well, the big deal is that the government has harshly punished those with similar thoughts," Cole informed. "Besides, Leo's family has thirty-three if we ever wanted to take a closer look," Cole slipped. Leo slapped him. They looked around again to see if anyone heard.

"You have thirty-three trees in your backyard?" Savannah said uncomfortably loud.

"Please. You have to keep this a secret," Leo begged, knowing he was going to be bending the law later that evening. "Maybe we can table this discussion for another time. A more private time," he suggested. And his friends respected his wishes as they finished up with lunch.

During sixth period, Leo saw Lucy pacing back and forth outside his science classroom. Then, he saw Mr. Holt pacing back and forth outside his science classroom. "Excuse me, Mr. Arnold, may I please use the restroom?" he went into the hallway to see what was up.

Lucy didn't give him time to question anything, "What are you doing telling people about the trees in our backyard? Mom and Dad told you to keep your mouth shut."

"It's spreading around the school like a wildfire. No pun intended, given the fact that parts of our planet are literally on fire due to us neglecting the environment," Mr. Holt rambled. "I have students asking about *you* in class."

"Cole slipped at lunch. He *was* the only one who knew," Leo regretted telling them.

"Well, now we're all implicated. I could get in *big* trouble," Mr. Holt didn't want to lose his teaching license.

"By drawing more attention to us, it will make later even harder," Lucy jabbed.

"I don't want to know," Mr. Holt walked away with his fingers clogging his eardrums. "La-la-la-la-la…"

"We sound like we're doing something illegal even though we have no control over this."

"We're going to be fine," Leo tried to calm Lucy. Before heading back into science class, he joked, "How do trees surf the internet? They log in."

"Not funny," Lucy was already walking away.

Chapter 11

Leo let the noise get the better of him. He perused his science class. Whispers may as well have been shouts; he felt the burning heat of so many sending dirty looks, their eyes glued to him. As he finished up his school day, anxiety built a home in his head and belly. He felt like his every movement—every thought—was being watched all of a sudden, not only by his peers but by the government, too. It was ironic because he was always being watched; everybody was. The government's use of myriad cameras and increased security measures—like a heightened presence of authority officers—aimed at keeping a closer eye on all of its citizens. Leo started to think that they were perhaps more like prisoners.

During eighth period, last period, Mr. Callahan gave his speech class an opportunity to reflect through writing. Mr. Callahan was a great human; Leo even contemplated confiding in him about the trees in the area. Still, he thought better of it; he needed to tread slower as his reality was shifting. Instead, he scribbled some rhymes down in his notebook to decompress:

Defeated
Depleted
Despite having everything that I'm needing
Confused
Mopey
Feel used
Not what I needed

Plan, retreated, deleted?
Or do I step up for what I believe in?
So many things I can't
Truly understand—

Achoo! Some smart aleck from class fake sneezed to mock Leo. "Sorry, Mr. Callahan. I can't stop tree-zing. I mean sneezing." The class chuckled.

Crinkle. He heard a piece of paper being ripped out of a notebook and crumpled up into a ball. As expected, it bopped him on the back of the shoulder and so delicately landed on his desk. He looked around; he was surprised it was from Cole; he opened it. Leo took a deep breath and repeated the mantra written on the paper by his best friend: *Be the change you wish to see.* He thought about his various roles in life and what was important to him. Friend, brother, son… and now, humanitarian. He then thought about his last few lines:

Plan, retreated, deleted?
Or do I step up for what I believe in?

Tonight couldn't get here soon enough.

Chapter 12

On the way home, the Oliver kids jammed out to the newly released, via stream, "Shake Your Butt-Butt But Don't Break My Button—THE REMIX!" And much like the original, it was fire. It pumped them up for tonight's mission.

As Leo pulled into the driveway and put the car in park, he felt obligated to say, "Listen, in all honesty, if you have any reservations about tonight, you need to let me know. I have made up my mind, but I can't have you risking your future on this."

"I'm in," Lewis's mind was made.

Lucy took the most time to consider. She bit her lip during her thinking process.

"I know you have the most to lose," Leo was referring to Lucy's college offers even though she was only a freshman in high school.

Lucy finally delivered her verdict, "I'm in. It has to be tonight. Plus, Mom and Dad are going to my school's early-planning college meeting this evening. It'll be our only opportunity."

"Hey, bro, when did Mom and Dad go to your college meeting?" Lewis poked fun at Leo's lack of certainty about his future.

"Not cool," Lucy slapped him on the arm.

"Let's do it then," Leo got out of the car. He circled the backyard, looking to let Autumn know they were home. Something told him she already knew.

As soon as Rosie and Ashton pulled out of the driveway, Autumn appeared. "Everyone ready?" she smiled.

"Perfect timing," Leo introduced Autumn to Lewis and Lucy.

Lewis used this opportunity to make the situation a bit more uncomfortable, "Nice to have you. I cannot remember the last time we hosted a fugitive on our property. The S.U.S.?"

"Yes," Autumn denied nothing.

"He's joking," Lucy tried to make light of the situation, explaining her brother's tendency to make things awkward.

"Well, let's get to moving. We only have a few hours," Leo suggested. "What are you thinking, Autumn?"

"I have been watching the area for over a week; there does not appear to be any government attention on the site. No cameras to my knowledge… none updated anyway," she finished reporting.

Lucy thought for a moment. "I can be the lookout. I have a pretty solid view from my bedroom window. You two should go get dressed in all black," she signaled her brothers to skedaddle.

"Don't forget these," Autumn hurled a pantyhose-type mask their way. "Just in case," she smiled.

Leo and Lewis sprinted around the house, toing and froing, trying to find some makeshift spy gear. For reasons unbeknown to the average person, Lewis used eye black although masks were provided. Leo *did* find some plastic gloves in the garage.

"We're back," he jolted a pair of gloves toward Autumn. "No fingerprints."

"Thanks! Great idea!" Autumn rarely forgot to cross a *t*.

"Places, everyone?" Lucy swayed toward the house, happy she was going to play lookout this round.

"Before we go, I just wanted to thank you for the risk you all are assuming," Autumn started. "I tried my best to spread the message. I think you get it. Everywhere seems to now have an eclectic mix of unpredictable weather: drought, harsh heat, harsh cold, harsh wind, and unreliable precipitation. The world is getting hotter. There are no trees to protect us from the sun. Fires just ignite back home. The land is being taken over by rising ocean levels. I can go on…"

"No need for that," Lewis interjected.

"Yeah, we get it. We're all in to help," Leo confirmed. "It's time to move!"

And with that, Lucy wandered upstairs with binoculars, making the most out of a view of the night sky.

Autumn led Lewis and Leo into the darkness of the area. Their terror was drowned out only by the sound of mating tadpoles in the distance, which proved louder than some acoustic rock concerts.

"Take it off until we're closer," Leo kept having to redirect Lewis, who was not able to see that well in the pantyhose-like mask.

"Stop messing around," Autumn handed them both miniature flashlights. Once they were at a seemingly specific point in the backyard, Autumn put on the brakes. "Here we are," she looked back at Lucy's bedroom, noticing the light was now on. Then it was off. "Lucy is in place."

"My phone is on," Leo confirmed, setting the volume to vibrate.

"Let's keep going," Lewis was not sure why they were stopped. But Autumn leaned down, grabbed what appeared to be a wooden handle and lifted a large chunk of grass.

"What the—" Leo speculated.

"Quickly," Autumn directed them into the underground tunnel. Immediately upon entry, Autumn closed the tunnel door she had been working on for weeks.

"This is incredible!" Leo pointed out. "You did *all* of this?"

"Yep! It really only became challenging after some buffoon hit me with a bat."

Lewis loved the sarcasm. "Smooth, B."

"This will lead us right up to the trees, the area, and I even discovered there is a shed. It might have some important documents we can use," Autumn led on.

"Like what?" Leo inquired.

Autumn wound up a larger flashlight and ignored the question. "Let's just get going."

The tunnel had five steps carved out of mud that led to a flatter, smoother surface. The large cylinder-like tunnel seemed to be nothing but a straight, dark abyss. "Here," Autumn handed the boys a bigger flashlight; several were placed periodically throughout various points of the tunnel. They were the wind-up flashlights. One side read: *Made in the S.U.S.* This was the first time the Oliver boys held a material from a foreign country.

The light they generated illuminated the perfectly carved crevices in the mud; the ridges were mesmerizing; it was as if Autumn was a sculptor.

"No service," Leo showed them his phone. Lucy would have to be crafty if needed.

"We're fine. We're here," Autumn signaled right above their heads.

"Another door?" Lewis questioned.

"Not yet," Autumn reached for a saw she hid earlier. "Here's the dilemma. I have only made significant contact with your side of the property. As soon as I cut this grass, the area's specific territory, I am not sure if alarms will sound."

"I got this," Leo's confidence struck Lewis and impressed Autumn. He grabbed the saw, knew what to do, and started digging the area above them. He went to work like a madman. Nothing broke his concentration; he was in his own world.

"He's been thinking about this moment for quite some time," Lewis smiled, defending his seemingly uncontrollable brother.

"Here," he handed it to Lewis for a bit. "I need a quick break."

Lewis went to work. Then Autumn assisted, proving to be helpful as she had just done this on the other side. After a few moments went by, "That should be enough," Autumn concluded. "Let's try it. Here goes nothing..."

Collectively, they slowly and gently lifted the large chunk of grass. They were met by a blockade. "To the side," Autumn reminded them they were under a shed. No alarms. They were met only by the continued sound of mating tadpoles. She poked her head above ground like a turtle poking their head from their shell. It was as dark as a movie-less movie theater. She broke the silence with a knock on the shed's wooden bottom. Again, no alarm. The three looked at each other and decided it was time to continue to cut their way into the shed.

They took turns until the wooden hole was wide enough to fit them inside. They helped each other up. The eerie shed was home to decades-old cobwebs, ancient-like farming tools and various hodgepodge planting pots.

"There!" Autumn pointed. It was a wooden chest. "Let's throw it down the tunnel."

"There's a lock on it," Lewis tried to rip it off.

"We can worry about that later," Leo shoved it down into the tunnel.

Autumn stared at the shed's door handle. She hesitated. "This is the moment of truth, I suppose." She stepped aside, giving way for Leo to do the honors.

He turned the black, iron handle and pushed half of the door open. No alarms. No sign of cameras. No blinking red lights. They stepped onto the soft, yellowing grass. The trees were all around them. *Thirty-three.* Leo had counted *thirty-three* so many times before. He was in the middle of the *thirty-three* now. The mix of conifers, varieties and sizes… seemed surreal. It was another world. These were not the same trees everyone had on their tree lawn. These were beautiful giants, standing tall for some greater purpose.

"Look at that moon," Autumn pointed.

"The stars, too," Lewis added.

"We have service again," Leo pointed to Lucy in the distance. She flicked her lights on and off to indicate she knew they made it. He gave a thumbs-up, knowing she would be using binoculars to see them.

They investigated the bark of the trees, making mental notes about the sizes, makeup and other notices of the beautiful standing creatures.

"We did it, B," Lewis and Leo did their handshake: waving their wrists, barely slapping fingers.

"Let's go!" Lewis replied in excitement.

"For real, let's go!" Autumn used the transition as an opportunity to hustle off the area. They turned the handle of the shed from the inside, making the area look untouched, like usual. They worked their way back through the tunnel and onto the Oliver's side of the property. All the way, they lugged the chest—which was heavier than Leo would ever admit—and made it out of the tunnel just in time to see Ashton and Rosie's headlights pull in the driveway.

Lucy rampantly texted:

They're home!

They're home!

They're home!

She tried texting several times, but the service was atrocious. The boys booked it into their basement. Out of breath, they messed up the studio, creating the illusion they were making music. Autumn stayed in the tunnel. They heard the garage door close. Ashton and Rosie entered the house.

Chapter 13

"Out of my way!" Rosie stormed in like a bull. Rosie was racing to the toilet.

Lucy was waiting in the kitchen. "What is wrong with you people?"

"Your mother's flatulence is out of control," Ashton waved his hand in front of his nose.

"Too much information!" Lucy made a bigger deal than usual. "Boys, they're home!" It was a good disguise to ensure they were inside and that anything they might have grabbed from the area had been hidden.

"Yeah, if you couldn't smell your mother," Ashton hollered while trying to hold back his laughter. The Oliver parents had a natural gift: not caring what their kids thought of them or how much they embarrassed them.

The boys were a bit out of character, not used to hiding what they did. Lucy was able to read the room, and before Rosie made her way out of the bathroom, she suggested the family watch a movie. That way her brothers didn't have to talk. If they didn't have to talk, they didn't have to lie. If they didn't have to lie, they might actually pull this thing off… forever.

The newest blockbuster was enjoyed by the Olivers like the old days: laughs, popcorn and someone snoring. When *Slow and the Placid 15* ended, Ashton and Rosie made their way upstairs.

"Don't stay up too late," Rosie suggested, knowing the kids would do whatever they wanted anyway.

"And don't let him sleep all night on the couch. He's sawing logs," Ashton threw his hands in the air, faking frustration for laughter.

"Nobody is sawing logs," Lucy cleverly joked and shot Leo a side smile.

Leo responded, "Good night, guys. We got him." Almost unbelievably, they got away with it.

As their parents made their way upstairs, the kids woke up Lewis and made their way down to the basement. Autumn was waiting at the back door.

Leo opened the sliding door. "Sorry, we had to play it cool."

Autumn smiled, "I noticed you watched the newest *Slow and Placid* flick.

Lewis made a strange face, "Creeper!" It made everyone laugh.

"I needed to be sure your parents weren't onto us," Autumn confessed.

Lucy mentioned, "I wasn't sure if movies were universal still."

"If it means the rich keep getting richer, they allow it. Some movies—and books—are banned. Not *Slow and Placid* installments though," Autumn revealed. "Anyway," she continued, "you'll never believe what I found in the chest from the shed." She yanked it inside, with Leo's assistance. In grabbing the chest, their hands grazed…again. That flame, that spark, was back and burning hotter than ever. It was painfully awkward as the two locked eyes and forgot where they were.

"Ahem," Lewis pretended to clear his throat in an effort to call the two back to reality.

Autumn shook her head. "Check this out," she pointed to an engraved *LOG* on the side of the chest. "It's my great-great-

great-great grandfather's."

"Wow!" Leo's eyebrows jumped to his hairline. "Her relative, Dr. Rea Log, figured out how to make recycled trees."

Autumn elaborated, "Yes, with the help of my great-great-great-great grandmother, Summer Log, and their research partner, Mike Etre."

Lucy questioned, "Recycled trees?"

Autumn pulled out the plans. It was all laid out for them. "The stumps you notice around town, we can regrow them into fully functioning trees again." She explained the process to them, as she had been reading through the letters, research findings and exploring items in the chest for the past several hours.

"This will help with the extreme weather?" Lewis wanted confirmation.

"It can," Lucy started. By this point, everyone was sifting through the information found in the chest. "Not only that, trees help with bouncing out excessive heat, turning carbon dioxide into oxygen, and will aid the rising sea level crisis. I know we don't know about life in coastal countries, but this will undoubtably help save homes, animals, and human lives."

"In Florida, in the S.U.S., that is the reality," Autumn shared.

Leo held up a notebook. "These have to be the directions." Autumn's nod confirmed. The green notebook Leo held was labeled in black permanent marker on the cover: *The Plan*. "There's a table of contents."

> *The Plan's Table of Contents:*
> *About Us ... 3*
> *Why we need to regrow trees ... 5*
> *How to regrow trees ... 15*

"Go to page 15," Lewis hurried Leo along.

"Okay, okay," Leo read aloud:

Any tree can regrow. In our time, we have regrown many ourselves. At one time we thought that this section of our findings would have the greatest number of pages. However, we have learned a simple and easy way to regrow trees.

First of all, any tree will regrow. It does not matter what part of the planet the tree inhabits. It does not matter the size of the tree. The tree will regrow back to the size it was when it was chopped down. Thanks to help from our dear friends, Dr. Salt and Mike Etre, we have tested and proven this regrowing method on thirty-three native trees on our property in Ohio, as well as over fifty trees outside of Ohio. Mike Etre has been arrested several times for his crazy antics in other countries trying to regrow trees, which he successfully did.

Of our thirty-three trees in our backyard, we have an eastern white pine, red pine, Norway spruce, baldcypress, chestnut oak, sycamore, silver maple, and sweetgum.

Leo skimmed a few pages. "Okay, here we go."

Any tree can regrow by taking all the material made from that tree, placing it at the stump, or bark area where the tree used to stand, covering all the materials with a tarp for just a few seconds, and unveiling the tarp. The trees will shoot to the sky no matter day or night. Both the sun and the moon illuminate, and the tree will rise toward it, even on days you can't see the sun or the moon.

"So the stumps around town are like our weapons in this

fight?" Lewis interrupted.

"Mr. Holt said the politicians were too cheap to remove them properly," Leo added.

Lucy added, "We need Mom. We can do this."

"What?" Autumn was an equal pie chart of shocked, confused, and excited.

"Nothing. Keep going," Leo didn't want to think of his parents intervening.

Autumn grabbed the notebook and kept going:

Two things I must warn you:

1. Once a tree is regrown, it CAN NOT be cut down!

2. Regrowing trees can turn into a form of art. It can be something that you master. We cut down the trees ourselves, made our own materials, and regrew them. It is worth noting, we also did this at a time when it was legal to do what you wanted on your property. We had privacy. I'm sure if you are reading this, things in the United States are a little different.

Future readers, please understand that the depleting number of trees is a crisis. Please set forth and try to regrow trees for any of the mentioned reasons from pages 5–15. It is the longest section because it is the most important, as trees have a multitude of reasons why they should be in plenty.

I imagine during your time, trees will be in even less supply. The government will have total control of decisions regarding trees. It will be hard to regrow them because it is nearly impossible to trace all the materials created from a single tree. Notice I did say nearly, not totally, impossible. If you see it in your heart to give it a try, please do so. I know all of our hard work trying to save the planet will not be for nothing. If not, I understand.

Best Wishes,
Rea and Summer Log

Autumn paused. Silence circulated throughout the group.

"Summer sounds hot," Lewis broke it.

Leo puckered his lips, now certain involving his parents was unavoidable.

"Told you…" Lucy was right as usual, "We need Mom. She can help locate those materials."

"Why don't we sleep on it and approach them about it in the morning," Lewis suggested.

"Sounds good to me," Autumn chirped.

Hope filled the air, but the lulls of uncertainty also sang. The Oliver kids set up Autumn for a comfortable evening in the basement and headed upstairs, all in agreement they would approach their parents tomorrow and come clean about what they had discovered.

The late night made for a later-than-wanted wake-up call. The only problem was that the wake-up call wasn't Ally or an alarm. Instead, it was the pounding on the Oliver front door that shook the entire family on a Saturday morning. Their isolated location on the cul-de-sac wasn't exactly inviting visitors unless otherwise planned.

Chapter 14

Pound! Pound! Pound!

Ally darted off and scurried under the bed into hiding. Leo darted off and scurried downstairs, in a state of confusion. His mind was a merry-go-round. Lucy and Lewis were on the steps, reluctant to join their parents at the front door.

"Kids!" Ashton hollered, ending their hesitation.

"What's going on?" Leo whispered as they walked toward the door.

"Authority officers," Lucy confirmed. "They probably know about last night."

Lewis didn't help, but added, "We're toast."

As the kids approached, Rosie wasted no time, "Did you kids go into the area last night?"

"What?" Lewis sounded shocked to be accused of such a thing. "It's fenced off… and it gives me the creeps."

"Well," an unfamiliar voice interjected, "someone went into the area last evening."

Another unfamiliar voice contributed to what the kids already knew, "And some stuff's missin'."

Ashton stepped into the living room with the two unfamiliar men. "Kids, this is Mayor Alder and—"

Ashton was interrupted, "And Puion Toll: Chief of Police."

The kids were sweating as if the actual sun was in the room; Leo's armpits were a shallow lake. The only saving grace was Ashton and Rosie. They were usually gung ho on being kind to, and definitely respecting authority. Although, this time, their demeanor was different. They were more annoyed and aggravated than concerned. Ashton said, "Okay, you overheard them. They weren't in the area last night. What else do you want?"

"Folks," Chief Toll began, "there was a breach… a break-in last evening. Of all places, the area next to your lovely home." Toll knew they were overstaying their welcome. Although kind of silly in nature, he was playing the role of a *good cop*. "I know it's wrong of me to assume it was you guys. It's just… we have no other leads. Nobody else is aware of the area given its location."

"Listen! We don't have time for games." Mayor Alder: *bad cop*. "You're the only ones who could've realistically—*illegally*—entered the area."

"That is awfully accusing, Mayor." Rosie put an end to the accusations quickly. "My children would do *nothing* like this. Even if they did, you have zero right to come into my house and speak pompously and in a condescending manner." Nobody messed with Rosie's kids.

"My apologies, Mrs. Oliver." Mayor Alder strutted around the living room. "Oh, it *is* within my rights to investigate illegal activity on my constituents' property. The stolen materials may lead to the alteration of our country."

"Or planet," Toll added.

All the while, the Oliver kids nodded along, trying their best not to show their hands. Leo kept peering out the windows, hoping the authority officers searching the grounds didn't find any traces of her.

Mayor Alder sat back in Ashton's chair and kicked his brown leather shoes up on their beloved coffee table. "You see, a scientist from long ago, a Dr. Rea Log, and his friends were curious about trees. People used to believe they were useful. Homes to animals–many even thought the survival of our planet depended on them. Ideas are no longer proven. Bottom line: these people tried to illegally regrow trees."

"Hence the area in your backyard," Toll chimed in as a side note. It was clearly unapproved by Mayor Alder, who was in the middle of a speech. "Proceed."

"The trees that were regrown were unable to be cut down again. *Hence* the area in your backyard," Mayor Alder shot an evil glare at Toll for stealing his line.

"So if the trees are a good thing, what's the matter if they're permanent?" Ashton inclined.

"It's not our place to decide what is good or bad for our country. That is up to the president and the government officials. That is why we elect them," Mayor Alder disputed.

"What would happen to the person if they tried to grow a tree with the stolen items?" Leo messed up.

"Interested all of a sudden?" Mayor Alder got the clue he was fishing for.

"Well?" Leo tried to gulp down the shakes playing pinball in his body.

"Well, young man, you'd end up on the country's most wanted list," Mayor Alder looked to Toll for confirmation. Toll nodded in agreement. "Just like our main suspect in this crime. Chief Toll, will you please show these children what our main suspect looks like?"

Toll took out a manilla folder. He removed an 8 X 10 photo and held it up for the family to see. "Recognize her?"

"No," Rosie and Ashton answered simultaneously as they genuinely studied it for a few seconds.

"Kids?" Alder looked at them.

Lewis shook his head; Lucy shook her head and shrugged her shoulders; Leo shook his head.

"Well, this is our main suspect: Autumn Log. Her great-great-great-great grandfather was that scientist I mentioned earlier. Be careful because that information in the shed is connected to her family's benefit; nobody else's, ya hear?" Mayor Alder didn't break eye contact with Leo as he and Toll made their way to the front door.

Silence settled in until Toll, Alder and all the authority officers made their way off the property.

Chapter 15

"Wow!" Ashton finally broke the silence. "What a way to start the weekend," he sarcastically pointed out. His face was red like a strawberry, furious.

"Do you have any idea what they are talking about?" Rosie gave them an opportunity to come clean.

"I saw her the other day when I stayed home from school," Leo folded.

"*Wow*, way to put up a tough fight, B," Lewis poked.

Rosie was shocked, "You *all* knew?"

"We did," Lucy confessed.

"Why didn't you say anything?" Ashton shook his head in confusion.

Nobody knew how to respond to that question—as the answer was painfully obvious. "We didn't want to get in trouble," Leo eventually reflected. "We definitely weren't going to tell those two bozos, Toll and Alder."

Rosie reminded them, "You can tell *us* anything."

A usual eye roll would follow, but this time the kids felt like that statement was true on big items, especially considering the way they responded to Alder and Toll.

"Well, that's good, because there she is," Lewis pointed to Autumn, who was hiding around the corner on the basement steps.

"Autumn?" Leo more so invited her to join than questioned if she was there.

"*Hi*," an awkward, uncertain Autumn approached. "I am so sorry this is happening."

"Mom, Dad, this is Autumn. Autumn, my parents," Leo introduced them.

"Nice to meet you," Ashton managed.

"Hi, dear," Rosie comforted. "Care to tell us what is going on?"

"How much time do you have?" Autumn smiled.

"Why don't we head into the kitchen? This will be better over coffee and breakfast," Ashton needed to calm his nerves.

"Yes, I am curious to hear more about your family," Rosie led the way.

Autumn filled them in on their activity in the area and built upon her family's history. The Oliver kids knew parts of it, but this time, she elaborated…

*

Second Flashback

The idea of *recycled trees* kept gaining momentum. However, the hospital got a new person to lead the financial oversights of projects. He went by Mr. Benjamin. He summoned Summer and Rea to his new window office. Dr. Salt warned them about him; they didn't see eye to eye on many things, if anything. He was taking over many of Dr. Salt's responsibilities, slowly pushing him out.

Rea extended his hand to meet him, but Mr. Benjamin didn't extend his.

"Well, as both of you know," Dr. Salt began the meeting, figuring he'd have to mediate, "your department requires quite a large sum of money to keep experimenting with *recycled trees*.

That being said, we think your program is *very* important. We are not cutting your program next year."

"Dr. Salt, if I may," interrupted Mr. Benjamin, not really concerned about butting in. "You have one year under my watch to prove something to me. I *promise* if you do not solve, fix, or show something *huge*—and I'm not talking about plastic trees, *huge*—I'm talking *huge, huge*," Mr. Benjamin showed with his hands, "then you will be shut down. You have until Christmas next year."

Summer began to fire back, "*Plastic trees?*" she paused and looked around the room. "*Plastic trees*? Clearly you don't know your head from a hole in the ground. We're not making plastic trees," fired a ticked off Summer.

"Plastic trees over stumps filled with material from that same tree, will soon recognize like-wood material and blossom back into its original form," stated Mr. Benjamin. "Then *pigs* will fly," he laughed sarcastically.

Rea couldn't take it anymore, "Look, Mr. Benjamin, there's no reason to treat us like idiots. We are aware of your deadlines. Understand that while it may seem crazy, the theory has produced some results. Just believe in us a little. All we need is time. This is something I have been developing for over a decade."

"Well, genius boy, you have one more year. That's 365 days," said Mr. Benjamin as he put his hands on the desk and leaned toward Rea.

Rea stood up, pointed toward the door, and Summer led the way out. Rea softly corrected, "365 and a quarter days."

Dr. Salt looked on almost hopelessly as they left the room, "You know they're good people. They're going to change the world. You should invest in them."

"Maybe. We will see. I don't want to be the bad guy. We just don't have the funds right now. I can't invest in maybes, Doctor Salt. I want to invest our money in helping patients."

"Then why is there a Moondollars, BFC, and McKing's in the lobby?"

"Please keep in mind that I *will* make the most money no matter what. Who cares that it's not good for people? When they get sick, they will pay us to fix them. It's simple; we're here for people. Ah, before you speak, please keep in mind I am your replacement, not your fill-in. I have been appointed by Governor Cashich and can fire you, kind sir," said a Grinch-like Mr. Benjamin.

Turned out their *Recycled Trees* were starting to show some progress. Albeit, it only regrew thirteen percent in six months.

"This is amazing!" Mike Etre announced, analyzing the roots as they started to recoil.

"This is *stunning*; maybe the craziest thing ever discovered," Dr. Salt admitted although reserved.

"What's wrong, Dr. Salt?" Summer asked.

"It's just that to closed-minded folks, like Benjamin, this isn't going to seem like much."

"We just need more time," Rea assured.

"You don't have it," Dr. Salt reluctantly relayed Benjamin's stubbornness. "It's not up to me. Benjamin will most likely cut your funding if something is not done immediately."

And so sparked the *all-or-nothing* tests. Nicko came by and led the reconstruction process. They cut trees down and made materials out of them: firewood, tools, spoons, whatever they could make with wood. They then placed all of those materials on the stump of the original tree it was made from. They wanted to see if there was any kind of regrowing when the wood had a different form.

"Maybe the tree's particles will recognize each other and regrow," Mike Etre hoped.

Dr. Salt came by the house. "Guys, Benjamin wants to meet in two weeks."

"It's only May, we still have a few months," Summer protested.

"I know. He's not very professional. It's most likely just a check-in," Dr. Salt looked at the experiments spread all over the backyard. "I can see there is actually progress."

"Yep, but we need to speed it up. We can revisit the design process if we need to," Mike Etre was determined to persevere.

"We'll present what we have to Benjamin and see what he has to say," Rea concluded.

On the day of the meeting, Mike Etre, Summer and Rea piled into their four-door hybrid and cruised to the hospital. Rea was ready to walk into the meeting, although he knew it probably wasn't going to fare well for them. Still, he was calm and collected. Summer, on the other hand, was doing a special breathing technique to calm her thoughts. She plugged one side of her nose with her index finger and inhaled through the open nostril. She switched her finger to the other nostril, plugged it, and exhaled through the one that she previously closed off… her best efforts to omit irate thoughts.

"Good luck, guys. This is going to be great!" Mike Etre was optimistic. He was in his last year of teaching; he could sense that the two were frightened, and it was his natural ability to calm down and motivate his students for over thirty-five years. He had never had to do that for Rea before, so he felt proud to be at the meeting.

A solemn secretary escorted them into the meeting room.

"Mr. Log. Let's get right into it," Mr. Benjamin started as soon as they entered, no salutations. "What evidence do you have that you can regrow trees? That's what you're claiming you can do, right?"

"Mr. Benjamin, good to see you again. Summer and I have been working from home for the last few months. Please let my team come in, have a seat and be introduced before the questioning summons." They all shook hands with other board members.

"All right Mr. Log, now that we're all buddies, let's answer the question that I asked moments ago. What evidence does your team have of trees regrowing?"

"Well, Summer and I have been heading this research project for two years. We have run countless tests in regrowing trees, as well as many other experiments that would result in benefitting the environment and human health. When we were given our "deadline" and threatened that something major better breakthrough, we turned our focus to regrowing trees after they had been cut down and used for something else. For example, the chair you are sitting on, if we planted the wood parts back with the stump of the tree that it was made from, along with all other materials made from the same tree, it would recognize the wood grain and regrow," Rea made great eye contact with everyone in the room.

Summer took over, "Rea and I conducted many of these experiments at our own science lab." She neglected to inform them it was also their backyard. She proceeded, "We looked to Mr. Mike Etre for some support. Mr. Etre is the Head of the

Science Department at Maplewood High School. Mike, would you like to tell everyone what you discovered while running similar experiments?"

"Thank you, Summer. I have been Head of the Science Department at Maplewood for nearly three decades. I actually had Rea as a student, although he ended up teaching me so much more than I could ever teach him," many people smiled. "You cannot go wrong letting this man lead you. He is something special. He gave me a call right when Mr. Benjamin asked him to do the impossible: produce an overnight stellar sensation to save our planet," Mike glared at Mr. Benjamin. "In my science classroom, I let students conduct experiments that involved cutting down conifers three feet in height, or smaller. We made wreaths and cut wooden logs out of the tree. The students sanded the logs in the woodshop class; we put our new material on the stumps in the school's backyard, where we cut down the trees. Something magical happened; the trees started to recognize our materials. They started to intertwine, and the tree is currently regrowing, back to its original form," said Mike as he raised his eyebrows.

"Is it fully regrown?" Mr. Benjamin pried.

"Not quite. Our hypothesis is that it will require more time to elapse in order to fully regrow. I can assure you there has been no greater breakthrough—scientifically speaking—in our world's profound history," Mike defended.

"Do you have proof that it will fully regrow?"

"All we need is time, Mr. Benjamin," Rea reiterated. "And all the materials from the tree. We performed trials after studying wood grains. We thought the splinters might recognize the original origins and want to reconnect."

"So wood, or *trees*, have a mind of their own?" The question was clearly rhetorical, as Mr. Benjamin rebuked such rhetoric. "Thanks for your time. *Please* get out of my office," he pointed toward the door.

"Thanks so much for—" Rea started to say.

"Goodbye," Mr. Benjamin interrupted.

The team was in accord: common sense thinking wasn't feasible at this moment. They exited, and just as they were about the leave the lobby, Mr. Benjamin came out to let them know they were fired and were told to never set foot in the hospital again. Unless, of course, there was an emergency and their insurance coverage was able to fully assume payment.

In the lobby, as Rea waited for Summer to use the bathroom, he noticed that he didn't even recognize the place anymore. There were many awards scattered throughout the lobby; he knew that they weren't for patient care; they were for making the most profit, which most hospitals would give to charities—but not Mr. Benjamin. They went directly into his bank account. He even fired doctors for being too productive; allowing patients to check out too soon was not fiscally responsible in Mr. Benjamin's eyes.

Rea noticed two roses on the lobby secretaries' desks. One red rose resembled most roses, red and beautifully open. The other rose, though, caught Rea's attention. It was reddish, yellow, and equally beautiful, if not more. It was different. Still in perfect shape, it stood nearly a foot tall in the recycled water bottle someone used to house both roses. Despite the fact both had been there the same amount of time, living in the same environment, the reddish-yellow rose didn't fully bloom. The scientist gave credence to the rose not blooming because that was the wrong place for the rose. Maybe the rose needed to be outside this hospital in order to fully grow and live up to its potential.

Chapter 16

"That's what my family is chasing. We believe trees are good, can be regrown and save the world," Autumn finally rested her lungs.

"That Mayor Alder made it seem like it was more selfish," Leo admitted.

"It's directly connected to my family. But, this... this is bigger than just my family," Autumn defended.

Ashton interjected, "We're with you, Autumn."

The Oliver kids' eyebrows raised like waves in the ocean.

Rosie confirmed, "Before we worked our way up the ladder at work, we believed in all the benefits of trees."

Lewis thought that was cool. "Well, we found a chest inside the shed. Autumn's hot grandma listed the many ways trees are helpful. For example, they helped protect our planet from disastrous weather, were homes for animals, a source of oxygen, and many more things," Lewis rattled off, feeling intelligent.

"Very good, son." Ashton was proud, yet balancing his frustration was still a skill he hadn't mastered, so the response seemed monotone.

Autumn laid out all of the findings on the table. Each person took a portion to cypher through. They made quite the team, especially with the help of Ashton and Rosie. Autumn knew her stuff inside and out; Lucy was a brainiac; Leo was ambitious; Lewis, well, he was the harum-scarum confidence the team needed.

Autumn unfolded the same map she showed Leo. Once she had a pen, she began marking it up, detailing her family's plan, as well as her plan while in Ohio. She educated the team on what the rest of the former United States currently looked like, uncertain if they knew. Then, she showed where her family was working. Together, they wrote in locations and taught one another about life in 2199, which was otherwise forbidden by any internet searches, from classrooms, writings, or any other form of personal or educational means.

"Florida is suffering right now. In fact, many people are beginning to rebel. We have no choice. Our land is shrinking," Autumn's palms up indicated her hopelessness.

"Are they making people live in areas the ocean already took over?" Rosie asked.

"Yes," Autumn nodded. "Not the safest living conditions with limited clean water and inconsistent power."

"This is what we were afraid of," Ashton rambled on about the history of Rosie and his career. Turns out, they were activists and once they started a family, had to take the jobs available in order to have healthcare; in order to survive. Ashton's blabbermouth aired his grievances with the government, citing how hamburgers used to be less than thirty dollars back in the day. The government's surmised a plan to combat immigration, making it nearly impossible to visit his own brother, who now lives in the New North—home to what was formerly known as New York. Rules included travel allowances only during four weeks per year; travel must fall on certain dates in order to cross the border between these two, now, allied nations: N.U.S. and New North.

Autumn empathized with his concerns. She went on to state her goal: to make it to Washington D.C. and regrow trees, hoping to prove to the president that trees are necessary. She then made a stretch that usually scared people off, but she claimed there was reason to believe that by the end of the year when it officially became 2200, Earth's atmosphere and the weather would be wicked enough to take the lives and homes of countless people. The struggle from polluted air and fighting for resources would become too much. She, her family and other allies aimed to regrow one thousand trees by the end of the year. If not, the way of life, and life in general, would hang in the balance. It was literally a matter of saving the planet.

"We have to help," Lucy doubled down.

"To an extent," Ashton nodded.

"We need to be all in," Leo fired back.

Rosie said what Ashton was thinking, "It's not that easy. When you're a parent you think of the ramifications of your decision-making. You know you'll be sent to the defense sector for the rest of your life should you get caught."

The government was hard on children. If you got in trouble with the law, you couldn't go to college. Without college, the only work they'd find would be in the defense program. If Leo got caught, he could be patrolling borders back and forth, thirty miles per day. Not to mention, he'd be a frontline soldier should there ever be a battle or war.

Autumn, again, able to empathize, suggested, "Why don't we let you two mull over some options? I am sure there are some reasonable ways to help without completely risking the safety of your family."

"That's what *your* family is doing," Lewis evoked.

"That was after considerations, taken by generations of family; it took us a long time to reckon with this life of danger for the betterment of others," Autumn validated the internal and external conflicts her family assumed with this way of living.

"Just give us some time to talk and think," Rosie pleaded. "Why don't you go enjoy the Saturday like normal kids? Might be the last one you'll have for a bit…"

Chapter 17

The Oliver kids planned to grill out for lunch, shoot some hoops and make up some songs. Lewis and Leo went outside first, but they had to rush back inside to stop Autumn from coming out. Authority officers circled the cul-de-sac, overseeing the *ICU Installations* installation of new cameras on the street, intentionally pointed at their house. It was a good thing they noticed them when they did.

Lucy beamed out her windows through her binoculars, trying to jot down the location of the miniature cameras barely visible to the naked eye.

"*Our cameras for your safety,*" Lewis poked fun at the saying their congressperson, Heather W. (pronounced DUB-YA), always harrumphed.

"Mom and Dad said they had to install more cameras and evolve technology because people were doing dangerous things," Lucy informed.

"Like taking weapons to school?" Autumn figured the idiocracy didn't stop at borderlines.

"Yeah," Leo was befuddled as much as anyone else with any amount of common sense.

In an effort to stick to the plan of enjoying the day, the kids ignored small-minded thinking that they couldn't control, and went down to the basement to have a good time. They played foosball and board games, and watched their favorite movie, *Together*, as they did every night in the summer. It was a feel-good comedy about people sticking with one another during difficult times. Ironically, it finally fit their lives.

Meanwhile, Ashton and Rosie mulled over their decisions and ways to best proceed. The family had dinner together later that evening, in which they opened the floor for discussion. The Oliver kids all voiced their opinion in giving up their normal lives and leading one more like the Logs. However, this on-the-run lifestyle, defying government laws, was a harder pill to swallow for the adults in charge, who were hesitant due to the potential ramifications should they get caught.

"We definitely want to help," Rosie cleared up. "I am going to try to get you a materials list for local trees from my work. We keep records of which trees are cut down and what they were used for. You will at least know what trees you have a chance at regrowing."

"That's awesome, Mom," Lucy respected her bravery.

"But after that," Ashton ended the joy, "we will be traveling to New York to stay with my brother. The travel window is open this week; we can leave midweek."

"I think—" Leo prepared his rebuttal but was cut off by Ashton.

"I know what you think. This is what it is," he sternly laid down the law. "New York, and the New North in general, is more progressive. We can try to see what type of movement exists there; we'll try our best to regrow trees like Autumn and her family. Chances are, we'll have an extended stay and come home when this blows over."

"Or we'll live on the run," Lewis provided the other side of the coin. This statement caused an awkward moment of silence because it was true.

"I'd like to stay with Autumn," Leo said between bites of his rigatoni pasta.

"Absolutely not," Ashton grinned, not really considering it at all.

Leo just kept eating, knowing it was no use. The plan had been set and it was stone, at least in Ashton's mind, and at least for now.

Chapter 18

Sunday went on much like Saturday; the Oliver kids introduced Autumn to all kinds of things they liked. They played their video game console, PX49, and had a blast racing against each other in various games. They sipped Caimanade, a sugar-less sports drink. Nonetheless, they even brushed their teeth, playfully mocking Autumn's great-great-great-great-great grandmother's seven-times-per-day brushing habits.

Later, they tapped out beats. Autumn's awful attempts at freestyle rapping lightened the room with positive, fun vibes. Laughter filled the air. Basic human needs were met, and Autumn felt recharged for the first time along her journey.

Monday morning came. The Olivers went to school, trying to remain as routine as possible. Leo touched base with Mr. Holt, Cole, Sierra and Savannah. He knew this would be goodbye, at least for some extended period of time. He was careful not to reveal any information that would compromise them. His support system may have been small but it was strong.

Before Ashton headed off to work, he embraced Rosie, knowing the severity of the task at hand. He lifted her up and encouraged her that she could do it. Rosie tried to approach the tough task as if it were a typical Monday.

When she entered the thirty-five-story building, she beelined for the elevator. She hit the button for the thirty-first floor and got off with the intention of downloading all materials from the *Resource Office* onto her jump drive. Her friend, Violet, worked on that floor and would be an alibi should she get caught.

The layout of the thirty-first floor was magnificent. Large, open glass windows outlined the workspace, and at the same time provided beautiful views of the Great Lake Erie. The carpet was freshly vacuumed; the cubicles were glass, most likely soundproof. Everyone was programmed to work so diligently that nobody noticed someone out of place, thankfully. Plus, there were so many people that it'd be impossible to know everyone.

Rosie continued her way through her maze until she noticed a huge room with a sign that read: *Main Frame Collaborative Space*. Violet always talked about it being a great place for teams to work. The open area, also outlined by glass windows, housed hundreds of cordless computers. Rosie slid into an unoccupied chair and wiggled the mouse of the computer. Luckily, a forgetful employee forgot to log off after their shift. On the desktop, there was an icon that read *Material Locations*. She double-clicked it. She inserted her jump drive, filtered through the lists, right-clicked, and sent all the pertinent information to her drive. *Three Minutes Remaining* appeared, announcing the remaining time for the data transfer. Rosie couldn't stop shaking her legs. Rosie also couldn't stop thinking about the employee she was taking advantage of. Her name was Aurora and she was the forgetful employee, even though there were reminders to sign out of computers plastered all over the walls and flashing on the monitors.

A few people entered through the doors and immediately took their seats leaving their G-pods in their ears and their eyes focused on their screens. Her stomach dropped when three women entered the room. She looked at the monitor. *Thirty Seconds Remaining*. A woman approached her; she was wearing a swipe card and her name appeared directly under her picture: Aurora. Rosie clicked the safely remove button and removed her drive. "Hello, good morning, Aurora?" Rosie extended her hand.

Confused, Aurora shook it. "May I help you?"

"Aurora, my name is Rita; I work for Mayor Alder. I merely came to remind you to always log off of your computer, especially in a shared space. We have files down at City Hall suggesting this is not the first occurrence," Rosie smiled. "We can assume that you know how to do so. Aurora, you should never forget, our taxpayers' money goes toward these signs," she pointed to them.

"Oh my, I'm so sorry," Aurora, and all citizens, feared the wrath of the government, even at the local level.

"It's no problem. Mayor Alder sent me over to make sure you weren't working twenty-four seven," Rosie chuckled. She was impressed and a bit shocked by her ability to bend the truth with such ease.

"It won't be a problem anymore. Thanks so much."

"Good day," Rosie nodded. She felt the eyes of those working in the shared space glued to her, as she made her exit.

When Roise was waiting for the elevator, and finally taking some deep belly breaths to calm her nerves, she heard a familiar voice, "Rosie?" It was her friend, Violet.

"Hi!"

"What are you doing here?" Violet was genuinely confused.

"I am so sorry. Please don't report this. You know I could lose my job. The elevator stopped on this floor, and I just wanted to invite you to dinner this weekend," Rosie countered.

"Sure," Violet smiled. "But you should just text me next time. You could get in far worse trouble than just being unemployed."

"Thank you," Rosie squeezed her hand. She gave up on the

elevator, walked right out of the door, down the steps, and onto the twenty-fifth floor to begin her workday. Nerves dashed around her body; focus was unfeasible. The day was stuck in quicksand, but when it finally ended, she raced home, relieved to see everyone's cars in the drive. Her mind finally relaxed for what felt like the first time that day.

Chapter 19

"Hi, Mom!" She was greeted by a fidgety-acting Lucy. "The boys made some type of racetrack in their room. They want you to see it."

"Really?" Rosie half-heartedly believed her. She could sense something was up. But, her faith and trust in her daughter led her to follow upstairs and into Leo's room. "What's going on in here?"

Instead of a racetrack, she found everyone in the bedroom. Something *was* up.

"What's going on?" Rosie's confusion turned to concern.

"You can tell her, Autumn," Ashton offered.

"Well," she started, "at first I thought Ally broke something downstairs. There was a crash, and I heard glass breaking. I was on my way to investigate; then I heard boots hit your hardwood floors and deep, muffled voices echoing in the living room."

"What? Who was it?" Rosie couldn't help herself.

There was a long pause before she revealed it was, "Alder and Toll."

"How can you be sure?" Rosie wanted to be certain.

"They took their time. They went down the basement, all over the first floor and when they made their way upstairs, I panicked. I took the baseball bat Leo hit me with," everyone glanced at Leo; he simply shrugged his shoulders, as Autumn continued before anyone could say anything smart-aleck-like or witty. "I threw it out of his window and made sure it hit part of the house. The noise spooked them. Toll yelled at Alder, calling him by name, to get out of the house. Toll asked Alder what to do about setting up the rest of the cameras."

"I took a nonchalant stroll around the house. I counted at least four cameras," Ashton was still in disbelief. This changed everything. Action would need to be more immediate.

"I can't believe anyone would do that to their own citizens," Lucy read the room, and she totally tried to instigate with that comment, knowing her parents might need a *shove* to be all in.

"Well," Rosie held up the jump drive. "I have some good news: I got all the materials needed to at least grow some trees. I had to pretend to work for Mayor Alder, but I got them!"

"That's incredible!" Autumn hoped her appreciation shone brightly.

Leo handed her an adaptor that allowed the jump drive to be plugged into her phone. Thousands of pages flooded her screen. The team collaborated to gather information for potential trees to regrow. The ones that made the most sense, and were worth the treacherous travel and task, appeared to be as follows:

Tree Lat/Long Coord:	Sent to:	Used as:
41.505/ -81.696	*Ohio Shipyard*	*Naval Ship*
40.150 / -82.967	*I-lockOH Goods*	*Dressers*
41.353 /-81.386	*Food Wet on the Land*	*Outdoor Patio*
41.319 / -81.346	*Maplewood Hospital*	*B.Wing Furniture*

"These are approximate coordinates," Rosie cautioned.

"I know where these places are, Mom," Leo reminded. "I'll be Autumn's guide."

Ashton shook his head. "We discussed this. You need to come to New York; we're going to stay with your uncle."

Lucy had enough, "Unbelievable, guys! This country sends its teenagers away to school with *insurmountable* student debt—or they force them to risk their lives on the border patrol force," her hands flailing, animated, at wits' end. "He's going to do what he wants in a few months anyway. It's clear you can't stop him." This outburst was unlike Lucy, but it carried a great amount of weight.

There was a bit of awkward silence only broken by Lewis, "I agree," he uttered monotonically.

"Me too," Rosie's stance caused Ashton to walk out of the room. "Don't worry; I'll talk to him. We leave tonight. Keep your voices down; the cameras have excellent audio. And you two, pack up," she ordered Lucy and Lewis as she left the room.

Autumn and Leo shared a relieved smile. They got to planning immediately, figuring they'd be on the run come sunup. Their best-laid plan would still be nearly impossible to pull off, but with the help of the materials list, they had a chance.

After some deliberation, Ashton and Rosie called the kids into Leo's room.

"Okay, here's the plan," Ashton started. "You kiddos will relax here while we pack up the car. We'll have to leave around two a.m. to ensure the dummy version of Leo we set up passes the border test. We're going to try to fake sneak Leo into the country to buy you more time."

"Wait, I'm staying?"

"That's what you want, yeah?" Ashton locked eyes with his son.

"Yeah," Leo nodded.

"We should arrive at the border check by six a.m.; it'll still be believable that all the kids would be sleeping," Rosie continued. "We'll try our best to let you know when we arrive, but I don't know how we can safely do so if they are onto us. We'll have to see."

"Oh my gosh! What is that?" Lewis saw a large doll version of Leo. "It's terrifying. But better looking than Leo."

"What?" Ashton could feel all eyes in the room were locked on him. "I had to improvise. We leave in a few hours. I'll stage him to look like a teenage-family-mooching lug who fell asleep in the backseat on the way to visit our family for a vacation. Border patrol might not notice."

"Nonetheless, you two should wake up with the sun," Rosie suggested. "You should start your mission of regrowing trees then."

"Yes, the journey of saving the planet continues with the sun," Autumn added. "I can't thank you all enough for the support and risk your family is willing to take. It does not go unnoticed."

Lucy offered an idea, "Why don't we have some dinner up here in Leo's room, play video games and laugh."

"I can make cheeseburgers," Leo suggested.

"But don't melt my cheese," Lewis reminded. The Oliver family had weird vibes about melted cheese. No backstory there... just facts.

"You still have ground beef here?" Autumn question. "We ran out many moons ago."

"They're veggie burgers, dear," Rosie explained. "And don't worry, *I* will be cooking the burgers. We'll bring up some fries and broccoli too."

The kids let their parents take care of them in their comfort zone for potentially the last time in the foreseeable future. They tried not to get too caught up in the moment. Instead, they trash-talked in a playful banter while racing the new SuperKart game on PX49. After sharing dinner and stories as a family, it was clear: Autumn fit right in. She was not the runaway fugitive that made Leo question or second-guess his choices for his family. Alder and Toll were way off; the world was way off. It was evident the entire family had faith in Autumn, and although this was the hardest choice they'd ever had to make, it was the right one. The *right thing* is a complex monster. Regardless, it was finally time the Olivers pursued the *right thing* on a level much larger than themselves.

After dinner, Lucy and Lewis packed some essentials; it was hard because they were uncertain how long they'd be away from home; they had to balance making this look like a natural vacation with a planet-saving mission. They were as discreet as possible, sneaking family heirlooms and jewelry inside secure spaces or wearing them in unsuspecting ways. Leo and Autumn had their clothes ready to go for the morning. Leo let Autumn borrow some of his clean clothes, and Lucy let Autumn sift through her closet. They all finally felt as ready as they were going to be. There was just enough time for the kids to doze off on the floor while watching *Together* for the millionth time.

Chapter 20

Bzzt. Bzzt. Bzzt. It was two a.m., and their cell phone alarms vibrated, letting them know it was time to move.

Leo hugged Lewis. "You sure this is what you want?" He made a final plea to his brother.

"I got this. You get that," Leo started their handshake.

"Love you. Don't get caught," Lucy hugged him.

Leo kissed her on the top of the head. "Keep them in line." Lucy nodded in agreement and took Ally with her to the car.

Rosie hugged Leo, wiped her tears away, kissed him and said, "I love you." Rosie, Lucy and Lewis hustled down the steps in silence and straight to the car. Ashton lingered a bit.

"Thanks, Dad," Leo could tell he wanted to say something but needed a jump-start.

"You know I believe in you and trust you; I am proud of you. It's just, one day you might understand—if you ever have children yourself," he looked behind him, trying to keep his emotions in check, at least for the volume of the cameras throughout the house. "You all mean more to us than you could ever imagine. Every moment away from you hurts. To think you'll be in constant danger grows an uncontrollable anxiety in my body. But I can handle that. You just handle the moments. Live in them; make the best decision you can, and please quit overthinking everything. You always have. No more making that face. I know it's you second-guessing and thinking of the ramifications. Just get to living. I love you."

Leo's eyes wallowed up with tears; he was only able to slap his dad on the shoulder and nod his head, indicating he heard everything. Ashton pulled him closer and kissed him on the inside of the neck. "I love you."

And just like that, the plan was in action. The car found its way off the cul-de-sac without any headlights.

Deep breaths were Leo's intended method of relaxation aimed at wrapping his head around the true magnitude of the situation. Words of advice marinated in his mind, especially finally being about to balance his feelings and thoughts with those closest to him.

Autumn overheard Leo's conversation with Ashton. She was wide awake. They both were. But they couldn't risk drawing more attention to the house with lights being on at two a.m.

"You okay?" Autumn asked.

"I'm fine," Leo settled down beside her.

"I just want you to know the feelings you are having right now are valid," Autumn knew exactly how he felt, and Leo knew that.

He simply smiled at the beautiful fugitive that blew his regular life out of the water. "It's just hard leaving them."

"They're great. I love them," Autumn smiled. "Even if they're a bit odd."

"What do you mean?"

"Cold cheese? Farts?"

Leo sighed, defenseless. "Yes, but we are fun."

"One way I coped was changing my mindset. That's what my parents told me life is: a mindset. Think about it like this: we can either bust our butts to try to buy more time with each other, or we can give up and only spend the next few months together. I cannot illustrate the severity of the situation."

"I know."

"You're probably just going to miss your girlfriend," Autumn tried to lighten the mood.

"Girlfriend? *Ha*." Leo pretend laughed.

Autumn just made the noise, "*Huh*."

Leo took the bait and asked her, "Do you have someone in Florida? Perhaps, a rebel leader in the cause to save the planet?" he teased.

"No… I don't."

"That's a shame," Leo said, then chuckled as quietly as he could.

"You're happy I'm all alone in this lonely world."

"*What*?" Leo elongated the word.

"You are!" Autumn accused.

"Why'd you ask me in the first place?" he didn't give her time to answer, "*Huh*?"

"I just wanted to know. You seem like a good guy and I figured you'd have one, that's all."

"Well, thank you. I'm just a good guy that's single."

"They remind me of home," Autumn pointed to the stars on his ceiling.

"Oh, yeah," he was a little embarrassed. "We put those up when we were really young. You must be terribly homesick," Leo tried to empathize.

"Yeah, it's hard," Autumn's eyes started to fill with tears. "It's gotten better since your family took me in though. I don't feel as lonely." She dabbed her eyes with the sweatshirt sleeves Leo lent her.

"Hey!" he joked, "Don't be ruining my hoodie."

"Sorry," Autumn laughed quietly.

"I'm playing. I'm glad you feel a little better since being

here. Hopefully, all goes well and we save the world. Then the government will realize we helped. The United States can reform, or at least we can visit each other!"

"That sounds perfect; who knows, you might be a New Yorker sooner than later," Autumn needed wishful thinking every once in a while.

"I never thought I'd see you this way. You always seem so strong, like nothing bothers you."

"I try to be strong," Autumn admitted.

"You're way stronger than me. My buddy, Cole, and I have two really cool friends named Sierra and Savannah. They taught us to reflect. Thinking, sharing, knowing yourself, having self-love and admitting fears are strong. Truth be told though, I'm kind of girly," Leo played around some more.

"I realized that. Lucky for you, I'm pansexual. I'm attracted to the person, not the manly or girliness."

"Awesome!" Leo just wanted a chance.

They continued their whisper conversation until Autumn began to twitch; she couldn't keep her eyes open. Even so, only moments after falling asleep, she was screaming in her dreams, "No! Don't!"

Leo shook her, afraid the cameras would pick up the noise. She was being really loud. "It's okay," he whispered. He took his hand and rubbed her back. He maneuvered his body close enough to hers, making it natural to cuddle her; it seemed to relax her. They were both lying on their side, facing each other. She fell back asleep, if she even woke up, not saying a word. Leo wanted to battle her bad dreams for her. But for now, rest was of the essence.

Chapter 21

Bzzt. Bzzt. Bzzt. Their cell phone woke them up at six a.m. Remembering to be cognizant of the cameras set up around the house, they had all their gear in their backpacks: supplies, tarps, snacks, miniature tools, and of course the USB with the tree material list. The final zip of their backpacks closing was their go signal.

They carefully bolted down the steps and out the garage door. It was silent... still early. They looked around the corner, trying to locate the speckled-sized cameras if possible. Technology advancements made it very tricky to get away with anything these days. They meticulously tiptoed—as if a natural reaction—until they were off of the Oliver property line.

From there, they dipped through holes in fences, ducked through peoples' backyards, and dodged early morning risers around the town. The good news: no citizen, friend, or neighbor would know they were up to no good. The bad news: the authority officers *would* know they were up to no good.

"What happens when we don't know where the cameras are?" Leo asked as he was trying to catch his breath as they ran through backyards.

"We just have to make them unsure if it was us or not. Don't stay in one place too long. Move with a purpose." Autumn hopped fences like a pro. "Keep up! We have seven more miles until we reach the hospital."

"What? It always seems like it's right around the corner."

The backyards around the neighborhood were so large that he didn't even know who lived in certain houses. Surely staying in the back and off of the streets would allow them a greater opportunity to stay away from the cameras, especially as more people made their way to work during the morning commute.

Autumn led Leo around his town as if it were *her* hometown. She led them through some tall grass that allowed them to hide and still have a clear view of the back of the hospital. It was just in time, too; Leo was toast from all the cardio.

"That's the wing, there?" Leo pointed.

"Yep! Okay, Rea claims that there were huge trees that were cut down for this newer wing of the hospital."

"So, it's in a hospital?"

"The wing was designed for that money-hungry guy, Benjamin. It seems like it was for personal use, not for patients. In fact, after closer examination, it's not even connected to the hospital's electric supply." She pointed at the generators in the distance that allowed wires to run to every part of the hospital except the wing.

"It's just a separate piece of the building that isn't used?"

"Right. The design is really unique. It's almost like a deck that overlooks the rest of the city. The stump from the original tree is underneath it still. You'd think after all these years they'd remove the stumps."

"According to Mr. Holt, they're rooted to the Earth. I guess they're really hard and expensive to remove. You saw the stump under the hospital?"

"Yeah, I was there before I came to your place."

"So we sneak down there and regrow a tree through a building?" Leo made her sound crazy.

"Harmless," she grinned.

Leo couldn't help but laugh. "All right. Let's do it!"

"Our best bet is to consider this particular tree was used specifically for all of the furniture inside the wing. It's that whole *use locally* thing. In Florida, we had to use our own resources for our own goods, too," Autumn, as if trying to convince herself, added, "I guess it makes most sense to transport goods the shortest distance possible in effort to increase profits."

Leo confirmed, "We break in, bring all the furniture to the stump, put a tarp over all of it, then reveal?"

Autumn grinned again. She was picking up on the fact that Leo was going to be an asset; plus, he was weak against her smile. "There is another tree next to it that we can do too if we have time."

"Do we have the materials?"

Autumn waved the USB. "Thanks to your mom, we do."

"Toll and Alder are going to get here faster than light."

"We're fine." Autumn removed her binoculars from her backpack. She glared through the windows. "What a shame."

"What?"

"Nobody even uses this wing; it must be all for exterior show."

"It does *look* good," Leo confessed, as he used his grandfather's binoculars to get a close-up.

"Let's go around to the west side of the building. There's a door that the custodial staff props open when they take their smoking breaks. We'll sneak through there."

They lunged over the strong, tall, yellow straw-like grass. Workers were already having a smoke. Once the overworked man, clearly not concerned with a thing, flicked his burnt cig in the air and went back inside, Leo and Autumn scurried to catch the door.

Autumn glared through the crack, "Nobody," she whispered. They entered. The open route led them to the kitchen, through the cafeteria area populated with people, and toward tunnels leading to any part of the hospital they'd like to explore. "Too easy."

"Benjamin Wing," Leo pointed.

They nonchalantly walked around the maze that was the hospital. As they approached the Benjamin Wing, a sign read: *Closed for Maintenance.*

"Perfect," Autumn said as she checked to make sure nobody was watching them. They passed the yellow cones, through the unlocked glass door.

They stood in the middle of one of the most divine rooms they had ever seen. The Benjamin Wing was a wide-open, perfect circle. There was a desk, fireplace, and enough couches to house a party of forty. There was a view of tall grasses and beautiful greens that went on forever; it was the most beautiful view of his hometown Leo had ever witnessed.

"Imagine the beauty if trees were still standing out there. The colors of the leaves at this time of the year," Leo's romanticized version of reality was enviable.

The sun painted a yellow, red, almost orange tint in the distance. "Even with no trees, no painter could've made such a beautiful masterpiece," Autumn proclaimed.

"How are we going to get everything outside without being noticed?" Leo asked. He was an out loud thinker in times of worry. Autumn, on the other hand, was a silent thinker. You could see her wheels turning inside her head. She always seemed to be one step ahead of the situation.

"There's a sliding door that leads out to a balcony. See?" They walked over. "I figure if we can hide in here until nighttime, we can launch items down onto the ground."

"Nobody will be here later? It's a hospital."

"The kitchen is closed from seven p.m. to seven a.m. No custodial workers will be here. They'd be the only employees monitoring this wing."

"Won't security be increased at night?" Leo annoyed Autumn.

"I think it's our best chance."

"I don't," Leo walked over to the balcony and looked down to the grass. "It's about a twenty-foot drop." He walked over to the fireplace, grabbed the firewood logs that had never been used, and walked over to the balcony. He gently hurled the materials over the balcony, sending them nosediving to the ground. They waited and listened. Nothing happened. Nobody came for them.

"What are you thinking?" Autumn wasn't certain they were in the clear.

"Look, the kitchen has machines running, workers talking. Doctors all have other things to focus on; plus, they're worlds away. And it's proven that if people hear a call for help when there are lots of people around, they figure someone else will help. Nobody takes responsibility until they have to."

"What, your buddy Mr. Holt teach you that?" Autumn joked.

"Callahan, actually. But thanks for taking such an interest in my personal life. I can tell you're digging me."

"Whatever. Help me with this," Autumn nodded toward the couch. The couch had an orange, suede fabric as the cover. It looked remarkably comfortable. The wood was on the bottom, on the legs, and on the couch's interior. They had to do some maneuvering through the sliding doors of the balcony. Once they got it through, they let it free-fall. The noise that it made upon impact with the grass was significantly lower than they expected.

"Not so bad, huh?"

"Shh," Autumn placed her pointer finger on her lips.

"We're in the clear. Let's keep moving."

Autumn checked the materials list constantly, trying to grab everything. There were four other couches they dumped off. They also tag teamed getting the oversized wooden desk off of the balcony. "There are only small things left. Get the chairs and frames," Autumn ordered.

The two teenage-soon-to-be outlaws therapeutically lofted everything wooden from the list, off the balcony, onto the grass. The materials were all near the stump, just as Dr. Rea Log urged.

"It seems we're ready. What did they use the smaller tree for? You mentioned it earlier?" Leo asked. Autumn didn't respond. Leo tried to rephrase his question: "Remember you said the furniture was made from this gigantic tree? Then you said the second tree we can regrow was made of something else…"

"It's the post that holds up the balcony side of this wing."

Leo's eyebrows shot to the top of his forehead. "We have to knock down the building and then regrow the tree? This place will be in a million pieces!"

"It's to help the world," Autumn rationalized.

Leo sighed. "Okay, let's do it."

They walked to the edge of the balcony. Stairs led them down to the ground. They took out their tarps, but Autumn took out a bonus tool: an axe. "I have a plan for the post; for the second tree." They worked all the materials into piles, scooting everything closest to the stump as possible.

Once things were seemingly in place, a thought crossed Leo's mind: "Are they going to be able to regrow even though something is above them? Like the deck, balcony thing. I mean you said that they shoot up to the sky or moon."

"*I* didn't say that. *Dr. Rea Log* did. We'll just have to try." Autumn maneuvered her way under the balcony. She ducked and struggled to get decent enough balance to attempt slicing off the post from the rest of the structure with the axe. Her attention to intricate details left them the best chance of regrowing the second tree. Once the first tree went up, the post would just be there for them.

Once satisfied, Autumn hiked back down to where Leo was frantically checking the time on his phone, mathematically mapping justifications of whether or not his family should be in New York by now.

Autumn offered his mind a break. "Our escape route…" Silence. She tried again, "Our escape route…" No bite.

"Hey," he finally came back to reality. "What is our escape route?"

Autumn, bewildered, let it go. "Through the tall grass and backyards."

Piecing the complexities together like a jigsaw puzzle, Leo posed, "Won't they just chase us on foot?"

"They have all this technology but can't track us if we stay off the roads. They didn't even have the area in your backyard under surveillance. They might not be as advanced or as secure as we're giving them credit for."

"Quick, get down."

Two employees appeared within their eyesight. They were literally throwing a football back and forth, one hundred feet away from them. If they paid any attention at all, they would've noticed all the furniture under the balcony. Thankfully, they were creatures of habit, and after what felt like an eternity, the employees returned inside the propped door.

"That was close," Autumn exhaled for the first time since

they started playing catch.

"Too close."

"Now would be a good time to do a final check," Autumn hinted toward the vacancy surrounding the door.

Leo nodded and proceeded to enter back into the *Benjamin Wing* while Autumn set out her tarp, hiding her excitement like a kid going down the steps on Christmas morning.

Leo's shoe hit the tile floor and he traced his way back into the *Benjamin Wing*. It was clear: they got all the materials and were ready.

Ding! He finally got the text he was hoping for. It was Ashton. He couldn't read the message; he suddenly had company.

"Hey, you!" an unfamiliar voice shouted. "Stop right there!"

Leo froze. In a fight-or-flight decision, he sprinted back through the door, past the cones, through the room, out the sliding glass doors and onto the balcony. "Do it! Do it! Let it grow!" Leo threw his arms in the air as he darted down the twenty-foot drop.

Autumn raced, slid and ripped the tarp off of the materials just as he leapt into the air. The balcony shook; it crumbled down like an avalanche; Autumn narrowly escaped the wreckage.

The two security officers in pursuit—huge guys—came to a halt. Everyone stared in witness: the tree shot up as fast as a rocket. Its branches pierced the wing. The security guards ran back to where they came from, screaming for backup.

Leo and Autumn were in a trance. A tree was standing in the middle of the *Benjamin Wing*. A ginormous, beautiful tree stood with gorgeous green, red and orange leaves, just waving in the middle of a building.

"Awesome!" Leo was mesmerized. "That's got to be over a hundred feet tall!"

"Quick, the post," Autumn pointed. Leo struggled to move the collapsed post close to the stump. "Hurry!" Autumn shouted. She used the axe to chop it into smaller pieces so it could better fit under the tarp.

Authority sirens wooed in the background. They both took an end of the tarp, covered the materials, and removed it in a matter of seconds. The smaller tree shot up just as quickly toward the sky, possessing equally beautiful leaves.

"Run!" Leo hollered. "Rea was right!"

They sprinted through and hurdled over tall grasses as if in an Olympic event. After a few minutes, they felt a safe enough distance away to take a recovery moment. They looked back to examine their work. The wing was completely sliced in half. The good news is that no working part of the hospital was phased. The taller tree looked like the parent of the smaller tree. Both trees stood proud like they were finally back home. Each tree curved slightly to the right, ironically causing peoples' heads to curve slightly to the right, unintentionally leading many to wonder: *what on Earth just happened*?

Chapter 22

"Nobody got hurt. No fires. No other damage to anything," Autumn tried to convince herself to feel better. "Only to the *Benjamin Wing*," they laughed while catching extra breaths by placing their hands on their knees.

"Beautiful colors. They must adapt to the season," Leo hypothesized.

"It's like they were never cut down." They awkwardly high-fived. "We should get back to your place and lay low. Maybe we can sneak back to the area to see if there is anything else that can help us show the government we are trying to do good."

"I'm not sure that's an option," Leo read the text that tipped off the hospital security. "My dad sent this text that expedited our regrow plan:

'Son, we made it to New York. The dummy version of you was just as good as the real one... LOLz. Your uncle has more connections than we knew. It seems Autumn's family has sparked revolutionary ideas in other countries, in that people are even willing to risk their lives. That is why you need to be careful. We didn't get stopped at the border, but people showed up at your uncle's house, looking for us. We are going to be on the run. Chances are, you're on the run. Stay safe. Stay heads-up. Make the best choices you can.'

And that's all," Leo made his face, clearly overtaken by anxious thoughts.

Autumn nodded her head and put her hand on Leo's back for

comfort. "That's really a good thing. They're not caught. We have to move though," Autumn gave him a push.

Before they knew it, the town was crawling with authority vehicles howling their sirens like a pack of coyotes. When they made it back to the house, it was swarming with authority officers as well.

"Split up. Look for any clues," a large, angry man shouted.

"Hide over here," Leo ducked down. "They're ex-athletes for sure."

"Oh my gosh, look at them," Autumn needed a new idea. "We'll never outrun them."

"We always seem to pull strings to get the star athletes to head security in this city," Leo informed.

"They're not the brightest in the bunch though, are they?" Autumn asked rhetorically. "Come on." She carefully led them around to the front of the house; guards were searching all over the area and property but neglected to cover the front yard. "You want to drive?" Autumn asked, suggesting they "borrow" one of the authority vehicles.

Leo scratched his head. "Why, yes, I do. But wait, wait, let me get your door."

"Why, thank you, kind authority sir."

Leo shifted the car into drive; this was a new low: stealing an authority officer's vehicle.

"Just go the speed limit so they don't get suspicious. More cars are coming to your house but we have tinted windows," Autumn was on her phone.

"What do you think, five minutes until they report the car stolen?" Leo guessed.

"Yep. There is one tree that we can restore within the next five minutes."

"Let's do it!"

"You're having fun, aren't you?"

"Maybe a little. I just can't believe this is actually happening!"

"You're doing so great!" Autumn looked at the sparkle in his eye. "Okay, well some of the trees in the area next to your house are what used to be called white poplar trees. They're your medium-sized trees. The one that I want to regrow next is a little smaller than the white poplar."

"What did we regrow back at the hospital?" Leo asked.

"The bigger one was a sycamore. They're pretty huge. The little guy, a sassafras. It'll be awesome to have those trees in Ohio's climate. Your climate used to be pretty cold and have wacky weather and these trees were very common. Now, it's mostly warm and moist. These trees wouldn't survive in this climate naturally. That's why regrowing is such an unstoppable force; each tree seems to adapt to its new habitat. The more diverse the tree population, the better."

Chrrch. "Mike, have you located the perpetrators yet? Over." *Chrrch.*

"Love the history lesson but what do I do?" Leo was freaking out as the car was talking to them over the walkie-talkie system.

"Keep it smooth. Keep driving. Do you know where the restaurant, *Food Wet on the Land* is?"

"Yeah, it's down by Fair Lake, an old amusement park," Leo responded.

"Great, head there. How far away are we?"

"Five minutes or less," Leo stepped on the gas a little harder.

"There's a swamp white oak tree that will tear the place to pieces."

"That place is pretty happening; it'll be filled with the lunch crowd."

"I know," Autumn picked up the cell phone that was left in the car. "Operator, can I please have the phone number for *Food Wet on the Land*?"

"I'll connect you," the operator spoke.

"Thanks." Autumn waited for someone to answer.

"Food Wet on the Land!" A hostess answered.

"Hello, my name is Steph McGeph. Evacuate the building now. I work with the Ohio Bomb Squad. We have reason to believe there is a bomb in your building."

Screams screeched through the phone.

"What are you doing?" Leo didn't want to add a bomb threat to the day's list of felonious activities.

"They can't get hurt!" Autumn exclaimed. "The wood from the patio fencing might injure people."

A computerized voice announced over the dispatch: *"Authority vehicle is stolen. Be on the lookout for a male and female, teenagers, driving a car with a gray-tinted exterior."*

Before they could make eye contact, Mayor Alder's voice projected through, interrupting the computer voice. "You two are going to prison forever."

"Ignore him," Autumn could tell Leo didn't know what to do. "Pull around the back, by the dumpster."

"Stolen authority vehicle has been located at 'Food Wet on the Land,'" the computerized voice spoke.

"Yay, they found us," Leo said sarcastically as he put the car in park.

"Get out," Autumn went behind the dumpster and grabbed a brick she had stored there days earlier.

"What are you doing?"

"We have to make a distraction. Everyone is outside," she

nodded for Leo to look at all the employees just standing around confused and nervous.

She laid the brick onto the gas pedal of the car. The car slowly crushed its way through the establishment, smashing through the glass windows, and only coming to a halt thanks to a massive silver stove in the kitchen. The tires continued to burn as people ran further and further away in fear.

"Let's move," Autumn took a shovel in her hand from behind the dumpster, threw another one Leo's way, and ran to the side of the restaurant that was not damaged, the side with the patio.

Leo could tell what she was trying to do and helped. They dug under the sides, trying to prop the patio fence free.

Authority officers' vehicles echoed in the distance; a herd was coming.

The patio fence wasn't very large. The fence had three wooden sides, and the bricks from the side of the restaurant served as a fourth, completing a rectangle. In total, there was roughly thirty feet of wood. They both used their shovels to try to prop up the posts from each end of the fence. Leo lifted one side in the air when he could. Almost simultaneously, Autumn used her shoe to drive down the shovel and propped her side of the patio fence out. Leo and Autumn moved closer together; the sides collapsed like the legs of a foldable table. They left the patio wood in one piece—not an easy feat, but they were each able to hold a side and move the wood as a whole.

"The stump is in the kitchen area!" Autumn shouted while walking backward, as they both balanced the fence. Autumn tried her best to stomp through the shattered mess the car destroyed. The tires were still spraying debris everywhere; holes in the flooring allowed some of the wetland water the restaurant covered to seep through.

"That's how it got its name. It was built over a wetland," Leo had a revelation.

"Yep, there's the stump."

"In the water?"

Autumn jumped into the ankle-high marsh. She put the wood on the stump and removed the tarp from her backpack.

"It's not going to be long enough," Leo grabbed the axe from his backpack. It took him five hacks, but he was able to quickly break down the longest part of the fence and get all of the wood under the tarp.

"It fits!" Autumn threw him one end of the black tarp.

"Ready!" Leo shouted as the wood was all covered.

"Pull it!" Autumn jumped out of the way as Leo yanked the tarp.

The swamp white oak gathered every splinter around and took off for the sky—well fifty feet in the air anyway. The small swamp tree tossed debris like confetti all over the bar and restaurant. The tree made itself at home, back in its habitat, standing leafless—for the season anyway, in a foot of water.

The admiration of the rare occasion was cut short by a myriad of authority officers screaming in unison, "Freeze!"

Leo and Autumn turned around. Guns were drawn on them; more than they could count.

Chapter 23

Leo's chin met his chest, as his head dropped.

"Hands up!" The authority officer ordered as they approached the teenagers. "Keep your hands on your head and walk that way." Guns served as the authority officer's nudge.

Leo and Autumn did just that. As they stepped away from the mess, drenched, they noticed around a dozen authority officers had their guns pointed at them.

Leo stopped walking. "Why are there so many guns on us? I'm not going over there."

"Shut the hell up, fugitive! Walk!" The same authority officer used the same nudging technique again.

"Don't push him," Autumn defended as her friend, or crush, or friend, or whatever, was being abused. She never felt more protective.

They were handcuffed in front of the patrons who now became spectators, waiting to see what happened. They were read their Miranda junior rights and thrown in the back of a black and white Maplewood authority car.

The same authority officer who pushed Leo drove the car away from the newly grown swamp white oak. He put on his flashing lights and siren, and sped off to the station. "There are a few people that would like to talk to you."

Nobody said anything.

They pulled into the police station and entered what looked like an interrogation room. It had a two-way mirror. The room was plain. As soon as they sat down on the cool, metal chairs, they were greeted by familiar faces: Mayor Alder and Chief of Police Toll.

"Well, well, well, looks like we were right, huh, Toll? You can leave," Mayor Alder said sarcastically, letting a manila folder gently fly to the table as he took a seat. "No, not you," as Leo motioned for the door. "The authority officers."

"You called it, Mr. Mayor," Toll chimed in. "Two fugitives in our custody."

"I want you two to take a look at these photos," Mayor Alder pulled out the photos from the manila folder. "Trees everywhere. How'd you do it?"

"We didn't do that, sir," Leo lied.

"Lying is a terrible quality in a person," the mayor glanced at Autumn, inferring they were a couple. "Does he lie to you often, sweetheart?"

Autumn was a stonewall, not responding at all.

"Don't patronize her. Don't call her sweetheart," Leo was done letting unbecoming behavior slide.

"Very well," Mayor Alder knew he wasn't getting anywhere. "We do have security footage of you two at the hospital. And at the restaurant. And leaving your house. Oh my, you guys can be convicted without saying a word."

Toll handed Mayor Alder a G-Pad: a flat screen that worked like a computer. "Footage ready for play, sir."

"Thanks, Chief," the mayor hit play and they watched the footage.

They had shots of Leo sneaking his head around the corner in the hospital, just before the guards chased him. They caught him red-handed; there was no denying it. Leo shook his head and couldn't help but smile a little because it was zoomed up right on him, unarguable evidence.

"That's you, huh?" Toll stated the obvious. He and Alder chuckled a little themselves.

"Oh, and wait, Autumn is that you placing a brick on the gas pedal and letting the car destroy one of my favorite restaurants?" Mayor Alder asked sarcastically, pointing at the tape.

"Alcoholic," Autumn accused.

"Just so you know, their food is great. And I haven't had a drink in my life. Watch who you judge."

Chief Toll's phone vibrated. He read a message and wrote something down on a sticky note. Mayor Alder read it and gave a head nod as if to say *thank you*.

"Well kids, the president of the New United States wants to meet you. Let's go outside. He wants to take a ride and see what you rascals got into today."

Chapter 24

The president didn't bother to get out of the limo. Instead, Mayor Alder, Chief Toll, Autumn and Leo entered the back of a long, hunter-green limousine that sped off immediately once the door closed.

"Mr. President, this is Leo Oliver and Autumn Log," Mayor Alder had the honor of introducing the two.

"Well, you two have been up to no good. I'm very disappointed that I had to make this trip," President Bill Jamen was not impressed.

The ride proved to be nothing but awkward silence for a few moments. Leo stared out the window. Autumn didn't stop glaring at the president. The president sent her some weird looks too, like she was crazy or something.

As the hospital became visible, Leo said, "What happened there?" referring to the *Benjamin Wing*; he was clearly still denying their involvement. Everyone in the car gawked at him for a few seconds as if he were a loon. Leo raised his eyebrows and looked toward the ground, embarrassed, knowing he struck a nerve and that his joke was definitely too soon.

The limo stopped, and everyone got out to further examine the grounds.

"The hospital was virtually unharmed," Chief Toll stated. "Just the wing. No people."

Thirty minutes or so went by as they investigated, walked around the hospital, and pondered the new addition. The first tall tree they regrew stood over one hundred feet high and its branches were spread out about twenty-five feet in all directions. The leaves were fitting colors for the fall season in Ohio. The bark of the tree was thick. Fire officers were trying with all their might to chop it down; it proved to be indestructible.

The smaller tree stood roughly forty feet tall and its branches extended nearly fifteen feet. The leaves were purple and beautiful. The bark was a lot thinner. In fact, President Jamen tried to wrap his hands around it; he could nearly do it. Still, fire officer axes were no good on this tree either. Dumbfounded was a good word choice to explain the feelings of the masses.

"You do know this is a felony?" President Jamen asked.

"What is? Helping the planet?" Autumn fired back with a healthy amount of attitude.

"Regrowing trees," President Jamen fired right back.

"We're not uneducated like you like your constituents. My great-great-great-great grandfather, Dr. Rea Log, is the reason for that area behind the Oliver's house," Autumn began to explain, although everyone already knew what she was talking about. "He found ways to regrow trees. Believe him now?" she asked rhetorically.

"Well, listen—" President Jamen tried to interject.

"No, you listen. Nobody listened to Dr. Rea Log during his time. We need trees. The crazy weather patterns, the changes in climates throughout the world, and the destruction of land and peoples' homes because of wildfires and rising ocean waters is a global emergency. I know I'm not teaching you anything new," Autumn paused for half of a Mississippi.

"Well, look—" President Jamen's tried again but to no avail.

"No, you look. These trees can help prevent severe storms, the destruction of property, and loss of animal habitats. They can impact peoples' health and well-being. Do you think because you're in a different country this is only *your* problem? It's not; it's the world's problem. With nobody talking to each other, who knows how long we have as a planet?" Autumn dreamt of this day every night: an opportunity to tell the different leaders of the world how she felt.

"Well—" President Jamen finally gave up as he was interrupted by Autumn, yet again.

"*Well*, Rea predicted that the world would be destroyed, a survival of the fittest, by the end of this year. When we bring in 2200, look out. In Florida, this past summer's storm season wiped out millions of homes. Where do we all go, sir? Leo and I are trying to save the world. So if helping the planet is a felony, we're guilty." Autumn finally took a few breaths.

Everyone was marinating her words. Truth be told, everyone was afraid of being cut off if they tried to say anything.

"Trees are not the only solution for the planet… in my opinion," President Jamen finally broke the silence.

Autumn put her head between her legs, ready to pull out her hair. "We have to do *something*!"

"Why make it mandatory for each yard to have *one* then?" Leo asked.

"Just in case of a shortage, we would always have some for materials," President Jamen answered matter-of-factly. "Plus, if we keep trees around, where will all my people live? What will we use in our everyday life? There are more people on the planet now than ever before. And I don't need to be a Chatty Cathy with neighboring traitors to know that. I believe trees were put here to be used."

"One per yard isn't enough. Man, it must be hard," Autumn started.

"What?" President Jamen was growing tired of Autumn.

"Living in denial. The mental workout your brain must endure to develop and continue to support that small-minded thinking must be extremely exhausting. You have to at least acknowledge these thoughts. They're hitting you in the face." She calmed to genuinely say, "We just want to help you."

President Jamen rolled his eyes, "You want a *thought*? If we based our decisions and actions on *thoughts*, we wouldn't be where we are today."

"You mean a divided nation on the brink of becoming extinct?" Leo never thought he'd speak to the president that way. "I'm sorry, sir," Leo looked down, knowing how disrespectful he and Autumn must appear.

President Jamen took a beat. "You know what, I honestly appreciate your concern. I see it's coming from a good place. Toll, take them back to the station. Have them kept in custody and tried as adults. They will pay the penalty for their actions. Besides that, no worries, I like that the youth is showing initiative."

"Mr. President, are you sure?" Mayor Alder challenged. This caused everyone to look up. It was uncomfortable, as the president made it known through his body language that second-guessing him was a rarity.

"I beg your pardon?"

"Sir, that's a minimum ten-year prison sentence. Now, these kids aren't normal. I know they broke the law but look at the power that's here. Trees were regrown. Indestructible. This is a weapon or advantage or something. That Dr. Rea Log is a magician. This power is profound."

"Mayor Alder, we plant trees *every*, *single*, *day*. There is no power in these hooligans' actions, I promise you," President

Jamen got back into the hunter-green limo and rolled down the window. "There are plenty of authority vehicles to take you back to the station. A heinous felony was committed by these two in your bailiwick, so I trust you'll take care of it as best I see fit. Now, I have a flight to catch. Thanks for hosting me here in Ohio." President Jamen clinked the roof off the limo twice with his gold pinky ring, queuing the limo to pull off.

Toll and Alder looked at each other, then at Autumn and Leo. Leo smiled, thinking they were starting to at least win them over.

Chapter 25

"Get in the car," Mayor Alder ordered.

Toll, Autumn, and Leo followed.

"You know he's mistaken!" Autumn yelled. She was at a cross between fury and hope, also thinking they were starting to win them over.

Toll and Alder's mood shifted dramatically.

"What do you guys know?" Leo finally called them out.

Toll and Alder's eyes met. They nodded, agreeing it was time to level with the teenagers. "It's evident that the world is struggling," Alder started. "We need to take action and change it. Dr. Log's ideas haven't been forgotten by everyone. We know all about your family, Autumn. Everyone thinks there's no communication between countries. That's a fallacy. We know exactly what you guys have been up to."

The shift in tone caused Autumn's mouth to open like a drawbridge.

"We take that information and run tests ourselves. Our scientists here in Ohio have concluded that your grandfather's predictions—that lack of trees—are going to end our planet in all the ways you've been saying," Toll added.

"Thank you!" Autumn leaned back into the seat, relieved someone finally saw what was smacking everyone in the face.

"Why don't you guys do something then?" Leo petitioned.

"It's an interesting predicament we're in," Toll defended.

"Yeah, if we go against our word now, people will have no

faith in the government. If access to supply and materials are changed, we don't know what'll happen," Alder reasoned. "Plus, you don't—well, *we* don't—have the support of *certain people*," he was referencing President Jamen.

"You know what will happen if you *don't* take action," Autumn reminded them.

Toll innocently asked, "Not entirely. Can you fill us in with everything you know?"

Autumn did just that. She recapped all the information she knew and learned since embarking on her odyssey. She concluded with, "The last thing I know about my great-great-great-great grandfather's regrowing efforts is…"

*

Final Flashback
"Do you wish to receive a picture message from Mike Etre?" Rea read aloud to Summer as they were enjoying the end of their delayed honeymoon. "It looks like a tiny tree."

"Babe, we can wait until we get home. We haven't taken a break from trying to regrow trees in years," pleaded Summer.

As soon as they got home, and just as they stepped out of the airport, Mike Etre came swerving through traffic, "Where have you guys been? I have major news!"

"What is it?" Summer couldn't help but smile.

"Get in! We're going to my classroom!" Mike flung the passenger door open from inside.

When they got there, they went to the back of the classroom. There were seven trees with materials gathered around their stumps and one small, but fully-grown tree… standing.

"Are you guys working with younger trees?" Rea asked

rhetorically.

Mike, still in shock, declared, "The one that is standing regrew instantly."

"What?" Summer was flabbergasted.

"Right before my eyes! Not just because it's young." Mike Etre was dumbfounded. "I don't know how else to explain this besides magic."

"What did you do differently?" Rea tried to wrap his mind around it.

"One of my students left their sweatshirt on the back table and it was covering the tree a little bit. I removed the sweatshirt, and it popped up instantly."

"Unbelievable!" Summer circled the tree in amazement, closely analyzing it.

"I left these ones for you. I didn't know what else to do," Mike pointed toward several other trees.

Rea covered one with the sweatshirt and then removed it. The tree shot up to its original two-foot size.

"Whoa, Nelly!" Mike shouted. "I told you! I told you!"

"Try pulling the tree out of the pot," Summer had a hunch.

Rea couldn't. "It won't budge. It's strong as can be," he grunted as he attempted one last all-or-nothing pull. "This little tree isn't going anywhere."

The next day, Rea and Summer gathered the team: Nicko and Maggie, Mike Etre, and a recently fired Dr. Salt. In efforts to validate what was produced in the classroom, large-scale experiments commenced.

They:
- chopped down trees on their property,
- made new materials out of them,
- gathered the materials near the stump,

- and covered them with a large tarp;
- they removed the tarp, and the tree shot to the sky.

"They must recognize sunlight," Rea theorized.

"They could be competing for sunlight," Summer piggybacked.

"I do remember reading about how trees in the rainforest are so tall because they compete with one another to get closest to the sun," Maggie chimed in.

"Whatever this is, it's incredible," Nicko jubilantly spoke with pride. "You did it, son." Nicko patted Rea on the back.

"Benjamin will love this," Dr. Salt added. "There is no denying it now. Plus, Benjamin has ties to the president of the United States. This will change the world."

They contacted Benjamin, the local arboretum, and word eventually spread to the president of the United States. Admittingly worried, yet hopefully optimistic, Dr. Salt attempted to set up the meeting. Dr. Salt's contacts from the hospital warned him it would be a longshot. As it so happened, Benjamin's poor influence spread all over the country; business seemed to play a hand in politics—a major downfall of the former United States. People acted selfishly for capital gain as opposed to truthfully doing what was in the best interest of its citizens. In hopes of keeping funding away from Rea's study, Benjamin dragged Rea's name through the mud to earn his team a worthless reputation. As a result, and despite Dr. Salt's best lobbying efforts, they couldn't get a meeting with anyone for months.

Luckily, by nature, the team didn't let the money-hungry scoundrels diminish their spirit. In the meantime, Mike Etre traveled the world, testing their work on trees in other climates. He visited many far-away small islands people rarely heard of, let alone populated. He'd sneak out of his hotel room at night to perform the experiments. There were a few instances in which Rea received a call during precarious hours of the night to electronically pay the fine that Mike owed for chopping down trees without permission. A phrase Mike would often mutter in a foreign jail sounded something like: *Here! Speak with my boss. He'll tell you; they'll grow back!* No matter the island and no matter the fine, Mike always seemed to get results: trees will grow back if all materials are replaced. They will take the same size they were when they were cut down. They will never be removed or chopped down again. This was just one example of how they furthered their understanding of the phenomenon.

Time flew and it was eventually time for the big meeting. On the ride over to the hospital, Dr. Salt shared his wisdom: "Time is a funny thing. Each second that ticks, we get *closer to* or *further from* our goals."

"Time is a scary thing," Nicko added. "Time is something people want to hold onto."

"Time is something people are afraid of, in fact, the only thing more frightening than time, is time lost," Maggie offered.

"Time is the greatest gift," Rea knew life was a mindset. "This *time*, we are ready to show the world that it's *time* for a change," he motivated his troops.

"I think it's time we move off of time," Mike Etre chuckled at himself.

All of a sudden, six red-orange bursts of light filled the sky. A white, tail-like streak followed each one. The former United States was under attack.

Frantic spread in less than a heartbeat. Rea revved the car, did an illegal U-turn and gathered everyone into their basement.

They plugged in the television to find out six missiles were fired from unidentified forces. Targets struck the North, the South, the East, and the West, and two missiles ripped apart the middle of the United States.

The president addressed the nation:

"American citizens, today we have been attacked by an unknown, evil, cowardly opponent. Like many things in life, we don't know why this happened or what caused these sick people to launch an attack on innocent citizens. Our allies are living in fear as well. There have been attacks in other countries, similar to the ones we witnessed today. This is unfair; yet, we won't back down. We refuse to let this divide our people or falter our way of life. We refuse to let such acts go unpunished; justice will be served. We will stand tall and survive. Please stay tuned; we will keep you posted with any new information. All we know as of now is that over eighty thousand people have been killed. More than imaginable are in hospitals. We have lost contact with the major cities as it seems they were the primary targets. We are doing an investigation as to what our country's total damage looks like. I am sorry I have no more words to say to try to comfort you in a time like this. Don't live in fear, just live smart for now. Life may look differently for a while. We urge you to stay inside your homes with your families."

Everyone was petrified. There was nothing random or juvenile about the attacks. They had targeted highly populated areas and government facilities. The president had no other choice—or resources to aid those in need—so the former United States now stood divided. Seven regions formed and operated as independent governing societies. Each lived peacefully with one another but had little contact. They were forced to be self-sufficient; they proved to operate better independently.

Therefore, citizens willingly and legally separated into seven different countries.

Needless to say, trees were put on the back burner. Life went on; families were made. Much like other periods throughout history, former ways of life were forgotten in order to adapt to newer ways. The dilemma of the time took precedence over any environmental consideration.

Soon enough, Dr. Rea Log earned multiple PhDs. He continued his work and was published multiple times for his studies on the impact the missiles had on the environment along with how people were affected from a health standpoint. He looked at the impact on hospitals, which were hit hard, forcing Benjamin to play a hand and invite Dr. Log for a meeting. Turns out, Benjamin had been promoted to operate as the New United States Public Health Director. He gave the president of the New United States Dr. Rea Log's name and set up a meeting between them.

Upon arrival in Washington D.C., Dr. Rea Log and his team were escorted to a dinner in their name. As they walked through the doors, it was clear no expense was spared on the lavish party.

"I'm nervous," Summer admitted, even after all these years.

"Don't be, it's only Benjamin. Oh, and the president of the New United States," Rea joked. "Etre, you sleepwalking?"

Mike Etre mumbled something about being old.

"Try being in your nineties," Dr. Salt shouted as he leaned on his cane.

"They'd be proud of us," Summer grabbed Rea's hand.

"I know, they're looking down on us tonight," Rea responded, hoping Maggie and Nicko—their spirits anyway—were going to help if they could.

After a brief meeting with the President, who seemed to be

on board and anxious to grow more trees, Mr. Benjamin appeared on stage. He tapped the microphone twice and announced, "People of the New United States, we know why we are here on this beautiful evening. Before we enjoy the steak and lobster dinner, let us give Dr. Rea Log and his team's lifelong work recognition," he led the audience in a forced round of applause. "Dr. Rea Log, how about a live demonstration? We are privy to your theories and have set up a workspace just outside." Not awaiting a response, he led everyone outside.

They found a tree near the entrance. An axe and tarp were supplied, confirming that Benjamin's challenge of a demonstration was not intended to be rhetorical.

Nonetheless, Rea met the occasion confidently. "Over the last few decades, we've mastered this," Rea took a hack. When the tree came tumbling down, Rea cut it into pieces. "It stinks being the only young person in the group," he made a few people laugh.

Summer took each piece of wood and placed it on the stump. Mike Etre and Dr. Salt covered the tree with a large, black tarp. Rea helped pull the tarp back, as everyone else got out of the way of what they thought would be a tree shooting up to the sky. Unfortunately, nothing happened.

"Dr. Log?" The president feared Rea didn't know diddly-squat about how to regrow trees.

"Sir, please," the team scrambled to figure out what went wrong.

"Still just blowing smoke," Mr. Benjamin ticked the roof of his mouth with his tongue and shook his head.

"Mr. President, please come to our house," Rea pleaded frantically. "We have regrown thirty-three trees on our property. Mike Etre has regrown several trees in other countries," Rea was growing uncharacteristically frustrated.

"I've seen enough," the president walked away.

Mr. Benjamin walked behind him with a humongous smile on his face.

"Maybe it's too dark," Dr. Salt offered.

"I've regrown at night!" Mike Etre barked.

"He did something," Summer was sure. She started after Benjamin, only to be stopped by a special security detail.

Rea took a deep breath and said, "We have given it our all. I'm proud of and love all of you. We tried. Let's go home."

Later that night, still in his clothes from the dinner, Rea ventured off into his backyard. He walked around the wetland and onto his neighbor's property. He chopped down a tree and made materials like he'd done so many times.

"Rea? Rea?" Summer came out looking for him. "It's three a.m., what are you doing?"

Rea removed the tarp.

Rea, sweating in his brownish khaki pants and unbuttoned, untucked, light-blue dress shirt, was staring in amazement toward the sky. Eight dim stars illuminated the blackness. They formed what looked like the letter C, an eye-lash-like shape. All of a sudden, one shined as bright as can be, then another, taking turns until they were all brighter than before. After a few seconds, the tree shot up toward the stars. There was a gentle breeze in the air as Summer and Rea locked hands, confident in what they had been doing most of their life.

Chapter 26

Alder slowly nodded his head and unknowingly stuck his tongue out to bite for a brief second. You could see his wheels turning, thinking hard. "Benjamin did something. But now, *we* are going to do something."

"What?" Leo asked, ecstatically.

"We're going to help you guys," Alder put the car in park. "Look, we agree trees need to be plentiful. We're going to let you go. We'll have to tell the president you escaped. He will most likely put a reward out for your heads. And," Alder reluctantly finished, "we may lose our jobs. If we keep our jobs, we can help you out in a multitude of ways," Alder reassured.

"What are you willing to do to help?" Autumn catechized.

"Well, for starters, I won't report the Oliver family sneaking into the New North—specifically New York, to President Jamen. Chances are, they're going to look for friends near Central Park and start regrowing," Alder proved he could be helpful and that he wasn't just blowing smoke. "I don't know how the president didn't know that. He's still not taking you seriously."

Toll handed Leo a walkie-talkie. "We can keep you informed if we hear any more about them. Not sure you should be talking to them directly."

"Thanks," Leo said in a sincere tone.

Looking at the rearview mirror, Alder gave him a head nod.

"These babies can be used anywhere in the country. Just ring if you need any help. It connects to us directly," Alder explained.

"In the meantime, can you answer me one question?"

"What's that?" Autumn answered a question with a question.

"What was Rosie getting from her work?" Alder wanted to know.

"You knew about that too, huh?" Autumn grinned.

"Yes, we saw the footage of her. She did well; it looked like she got what she needed," Alder acknowledged.

"They're the materials list needed to regrow trees," Leo confessed. "I'm hoping she can somehow access similar lists outside of Ohio."

Toll divulged, "I think she has more access than you think. She signed into her work account from New York. I hope she has the information digitally."

"Wow! That's good news!" Leo affirmed.

"Listen," Alder put the car in park. "We're going to go inside and play it cool. But just know, everyone's lives are now changed forever."

They filed out of the four-door authority vehicle and headed into Alder's house to spend the rest of the night collaborating.

Chapter 27

"Wow, being mayor really pays the bills, eh?" Autumn commented on Alder's incredible home.

"Yeah, you can't hide money!" Leo joked. But honestly, Alder's house was legit. He had a stone home, and a beautiful tree on the tree lawn like every other resident, and when they walked inside, it felt like they were headed to the Royal Ball or something. A large chandelier lit the open foyer; wooden floors shined with cleanliness; a spacious study with books and desks became their research headquarters for the evening.

Alder supplied them with drinks and food, figuring they'd need to fuel up before venturing out to try to regrow trees outside of Maplewood. Toll made some phone calls while the two teens mapped out their route and ensured the material lists downloaded to Autumn's phone, just in case they'd lose service.

Eventually, Toll reported back: "Lewis, Lucy, Rosie, and Ashton are going to start regrowing some trees in Central Park." Toll went on to explain that he knew they were in good hands. "It is worth noting, the park is now a breeding ground for unhoused people and crime. At one time it was one of the most beautiful places on the planet. Now, authorities are reluctant to step foot in the park."

Alder eased worries a bit, "All that means is they won't get caught."

"That's dangerous though," Leo couldn't disguise his concern.

"Central Park is a zoo. They create their own rules, a survival of the fittest already. No worries; they'll be well equipped and many people will help them," Toll winked to make Leo feel better.

Alder reckoned, "So Central Park is covered. We need to keep focus on Ohio; it has the lowest population and a greater number of stumps to regrow compared to many other states."

They started picking the biggest trees they could find in order to draw the most attention. Their list included: hickory trees, red oaks and white pine trees. They were used for cabins at a campground in central Ohio, *Groveland Camping Resorts*.

"This will be perfect. The cabins are close enough to one another, yet spaced out so nobody will get to us too quickly. Those *will* be manageable," Leo was familiar with the campground from his childhood.

"Okay, that's what we'll do, Leo," Autumn declared.

"Sounds good, Autumn," Leo rethought what he said immediately. It's funny how people rarely use first names when they're together so much. "Usually, I call my family nicknames. It sounds weird calling you Autumn."

"I felt like you were mad at me or something," she smiled.

They continued planning their route. They passed around pertinent information, studied Rea and Summer's tree-regrowing guide and even taught Toll and Alder how to regrow.

"We'll start in the morning," Alder notified, thinking he had the process under control. "We'll handle trees around here if we can."

"We're going to head off to Groveland, then—," Autumn was nudged discreetly by Leo.

"From there, we'll contact you," Leo finished Autumn's sentence. "Not that we don't trust you, but it might just be better for everyone if we don't share every detail about our whereabouts," Leo offered.

Toll agreed and added, "In order to remain incognito, we'll have to announce your "escape" at nine a.m., when the courthouse opens. President Jamen will put out a reward for your head. For the most part, you'll just have to watch out for money-hungry citizens. Vigilantes, if you will. The authorities that we have close relationships with have been contacted, so you'll have friends in certain areas."

"Be afraid and weary of the locals. Especially at Groveland. There are people who live there year-round," Alder warned. "Traditionalists who love their land—and *their* reality—and won't take kindly to you changing it."

"We'd be improving their land," Autumn insisted, confused. "The trees can be natural resources again, even after they've been used; what is the harm?"

Toll spoke, "You just don't get it yet. You're kids that have this vision that everyone sees things your way. People don't know you guys are trying to help them; they don't know any better. Few people on the planet know better. Many are still stuck in the caves, chained, watching shadows. After all, perception is reality."

Leo remembered that phrase from Mr. Holt's class, but Autumn had no idea what he was talking about.

Alder could tell. "Just tread with caution. The government made it their goal for people to fear trees, leading them to believe they harmed the well-being of the country. It's going to be hard to convince them of a different truth, especially with no tangible evidence that the world will end in a couple of months."

Leo nodded, indicating he understood. "Thanks so much for everything... for putting cameras in my house, for breaking my window," Toll and Alder laughed at Leo. "But honestly, thanks," Leo gave them solid eye contact and a nod.

"Good luck, wild child," Toll smiled and shook their hands.

"Be careful. Let me know if you need anything. Remember, you two will be reported missing at nine a.m. That'll give you a nine-hour head start," Alder calculated as he examined his watch. "It's nearly midnight."

They became reacquainted with their backpacks, adjusted the straps, and were ready to burst out the door. Leo and Autumn hit the sleeping suburb running. Not a soul was out on the town.

Chapter 28

"Groveland is usually a two-hour drive," Leo mustered between deep breaths, as they were beginning to pick up the pace.

"We're going to have to find a place to get a bit of shut-eye," Autumn suggested.

"I have a plan."

They made their way twelve miles south of Maplewood. Signs for *Kant State University* let Autumn in on Leo's plan.

"Kant State?" Autumn was taken by the name. "Who would name something *Kant State*? A school?" she laughed. "Kant read, Kant write."

"Yeah, we get it," Leo huffed. "Those jokes have been around forever. Truth be told, it's a great school."

"Oh, I get it," Autumn figured it out. "That's where you're going next year, ya know, if we can save the world."

"Maybe," Leo buried his hurt feelings as best he could. "We should rest here."

"Why would we stop here? It's gotta be two a.m. and people are still out. Authorities are swarming."

"Hiding in plain sight," Leo mustered between deep breaths again. "Why would they look for us? Our pictures aren't out anywhere. Plus, we're still in custody, remember?"

Autumn raised her eyebrows, "Good point."

"We can get some sleep behind this huge rock, on some benches I saw when I took a tour. I remember how to get there. Nobody will find us when it's this dark."

Campus proved to be a party scene: house after house blared music and littered their lawns with empty plastic cups. They didn't have to try hard to blend in. Most students made a scene of themselves with loud, distracting, eye-catching behavior. Campus authority officers seemed to let certain things go for some reason. Students were certainly breaking myriad laws.

"Funny how people say they're at school but spend the majority of the time out of class," Autumn hypothesized based on observations.

"It is two-thirty a.m.," Leo reminded her.

"I know; it's still weird to me. People can party all hours of the night and knowingly break the law, even though everyone knows it—including authority officers, and it still goes on. But we regrow a couple of little trees and—" Autumn was interrupted.

"They were huge trees!"

She ignored Leo, "And the president disciplines us in his car? That's messed up."

Truth be told, Leo agreed. "Look, I talk about this with my people all the time. What is the incentive for doing the right thing? Our country needs to ask itself that. It's frustrating, but we have to make the most of our moments."

"True. My dad always says: *can't get today back.*"

"I love it!" Leo really did. "Oh, look, there's the Psychology Department."

They entered a courtyard-like seating area. Atop a hill stood a huge brain carved out of brownish-red stone. The indents on the statue were so detailed that the replica looked almost too real. Large grasses surrounded benches and study areas, while fences surrounded the area as a layer of extra protection for the night's rest. They settled into separate benches for the night.

"This is what I would study if I came here next year."

"Cool!" Autumn sprawled out and yanked the thinnest blanket ever from her backpack. "So, a therapist?" she guessed.

"Yep!"

"Why'd you choose that?"

"I feel like that's where the real change happens for people. Everyone is so afraid of therapy but not guns. They're more terrified of themselves. I want to help people rearrange that mindset to see mental health is not something you fix but rather practice. It extends to your diet, exercise and stress levels. There are so many factors. I'm tired of hearing about mental illness and fixes from people who do not understand what mental health even is."

Autumn could tell he was passionate, but he was also getting a little too fired up before some much needed shut-eye. "I like that. It makes total sense to me." Autumn tried to change the subject, "It's the perfect temperature to sleep in, don't you think? This Ohio weather is way cooler than Florida's."

"The breeze is a little cool," Leo responded, blanketless.

"Just as I get comfortable," Autumn responded in a playful manner. She walked over to the bench Leo was on and scooted him over. They spooned on the black, cool, iron bench.

Leo could only smile. He was secretly hoping she would do that, but would never ask her to. He put his arm around her.

"Watch it."

"It's just to conserve space. We can't fit if I don't," Leo couldn't hide his joy.

"You think you're smooth, don't you?" Autumn flirted.

Leo raised his eyebrows, smiled huge, and closed his eyes. "Good night."

The flirtation ended abruptly as Autumn quickly drifted to

sleep. Her shakes took over again. Leo held her, wondering what she could be dreaming about: regrowing trees, punching the president in the face, or maybe dinner and a movie with him after they save the planet. Who knows? He couldn't fall asleep. He gazed up at the cloudless sky as his mind took over. He thought about how it would be a good day to travel in the morning. Like a kid skipping rocks in the water, his mind skipped thoughts from his childhood throughout his head. Like how a clear sky at night meant delight, the next day. He wondered if he noticed as many clouds in the sky anymore. He felt like he noticed way more when he was growing up. Rosie would always say clouds were dancing across the blue ceiling. Sometimes they called the sky an upside-down ocean. If only he could live in that reality forever.

He tried his deep breathing technique because his thoughts were making him make his face again—it'd crunch up and look like he was painfully smiling. The breathing did help after a bit of time. He looked at Autumn; that calmed him as well.

He looked up; the real stars proved to be just as bright as the stars on his ceiling back home. He thought of his family some more. His brother and sister's favorite stars were these two bright ones and the moon. They always seemed to connect, one right over the other. They always joked that if you connected them it'd look like a curved fingernail. He stared at the stars until he eventually fell asleep.

Chapter 29

"Wake up, fools!" Two men were cleaning the campus. They thought Autumn and Leo were students who partied too hard. "Kids don't appreciate anything anymore. They're lazy animals. Sloofs!"

"Sir, we were just resting. Sorry," Leo managed to mumble while rubbing his eyes.

As they were shooed off, Autumn admitted, "I feel pretty good."

"Yeah, who'd thought sleeping on a bench would be so rejuvenating?" They shared a smile. "I guess most girls would love to fall asleep in my arms, though," he joked.

Autumn imitated him, pretending to laugh like he did. "We should get going. We have to cover seventy-five miles or so today."

She pulled out her compass. "Let's head south. We should run periodically, while nobody thinks it's suspicious. Make it look like we're working out."

They broke into a jog and continued their odyssey. They came across some old shops in the old college town. "That's it," Leo broke off route to approach *Old and Bold*, a thrift store. "Excuse me, do you sell watches?" he addressed the clerk as he lifted the gate to open the store for the day.

"Yes, we do. Cheapest one runs ya' two hundred bones," the employee answered.

They had no money. Autumn pulled Leo's arm. "We don't

have any money. Why do we need watches?"

"They'll be able to track us with our phones once we're reported this morning. We'll need to be in sync with each other."

"Fine," Autumn turned her attention back to the employee. "That's a fine price, but what can we do to convince you to give us that watch for free?"

He chuckled, "Nothing is free, buddy."

"What if we show you a magic trick that will blow your mind?" Leo asked.

"No, Leo!" Autumn barked.

"Who's Leo? This girl is nuts; I'm Jason," Leo shook the clerk's hand.

"I'm Phoenix, and I love magic."

"We need a watch," Leo reminded. He walked over to Autumn and whispered, "Stop using real names. And plus—we can regrow a little guy. It won't take long. We can look it up in the materials list. There has to be materials around here. There are stumps all over town."

Autumn sifted through the possibilities while Leo and Phoenix made small talk. She finally located some materials outside a local theater. The theater was in sight from the thrift store. It had wooden benches outside. She gave Leo the head nod, indicating she was ready. She headed for the theater benches.

Leo put the watch on his wrist. As he buckled the black band and closely examined the silver, rectangular face, he said, "All right then, come this way. You see, Phoenix, we can regrow trees. Don't tell anyone, please. Aileen," Leo handed it over to Autumn, continuing to use aliases.

"Thank you, Jason. That theatre up ahead is next to a mahogany stump. It's not the biggest tree ever. The materials from that tree were used to build these benches on the sidewalk."

Autumn signaled for help lifting the eight benches scattered along the sidewalk. "You're lucky it's a ghost town," she whispered to Leo. They smiled, going with the flow.

They moved the benches around the stump, made sure all the materials were close together, and covered them with their tarp. They looked around to make sure nobody was watching besides the eccentric employee, Phoenix, and they removed the tarp. The tree shot up; everyone ducked for cover as screws from the wood went flying into the street, denting cars, hitting buildings and shattering glass.

The tree jumped up to be nine feet tall. Red and green leaves hung from the four thin branches with pride. *KSU 2010* was carved into the tree's bark.

The employee's jaw dropped down like a drawbridge; he stood back, speechless... amazed. He shook his head, took off his glasses and shot the craziest look in their direction. He was losing his mind. He began laughing hysterically.

"Let's go!" Autumn demanded. "We totally messed with him; he's losing it!"

"We needed the watches." Leo approached him, "Hey, man; it's all right; you okay?"

Autumn stood from a distance, inching further from the situation as more and more people gathered into the street, anxious to find out what in the world just happened.

"How was that possible?" Phoenix finally blubbered.

"Phoenix, let's go inside the store," Leo led him back inside *Old and Bold*. "This is a nice store, is it yours?"

"Yes," Phoenix spat, still shaking. "Owned it for twenty-five years."

"Very good," Leo sat the man down on the windowsill. "Deep breaths, pal, deep breaths."

It took a few moments but Phoenix finally calmed down. "You know I've heard people could regrow trees. It has been a myth here ever since I could remember."

"Really?" Leo played dumb.

"Yeah, some old scientists from around these parts, I guess…"

"We have it figured out pretty well. That's now four total trees we've regrown so far," Leo slipped.

"Four? So far? You're not done yet?" Phoenix asked, shocked.

"Not yet, sir. We're on a mission. If there aren't enough trees on the planet by New Year's we think the planet will self-destruct."

"How many?"

"It's hard to say because we don't know how many trees are standing in other countries and on other continents. Regardless, we're on a mission to rescue as many as we can."

"Can I help?"

"Phoenix, we'd love your help. Unfortunately, we're on our way out of town."

"What? Stay!"

"We can't."

"There are trees to be regrown here!"

"We've already been captured and escaped. We must flee."

"Please, please, take some goodies," Phoenix flailed his arms in the air. He grabbed some bottled water, the other watch and two bike helmets!

"Phoenix, are you serious?" Leo was overwhelmed by his generosity.

"Yes, yes, please. Anything I can do to help," Phoenix smiled. "I hope the bikes help. Good luck!" Leo went to say something but Phoenix interrupted, "Don't worry, Leo, I didn't see anything," he winked. Phoenix was no dummy.

Autumn, now way up the road, was signaling to hurry it along; authority officers were in the distance. Leo signaled to her to hurry back, holding up their bike helmets. She hurried over once she saw. Autumn waved to Phoenix—who was leaning against the store window, with a newfound calm over him, watching them get ready.

They clicked their helmets under their chins; Autumn led the way. They casually walked their bikes past the authority officers on the scene. Autumn found a flight of stone steps that led them down to a sidewalk that ran alongside a stream of flowing water. The stream flowed around curves with no end in sight. They began to ride on the sidewalk, a stream on their left and railroad tracks even further to their left, running parallel with the water.

Chapter 30

The bike path was a blessing. They peddled past picnic tables, built-in grills and some optimistic graffiti writings sprayed on run-down buildings. It wouldn't look suspicious that they were biking. The path felt secluded, private, and safe. On top of that, there were maps highlighting different routes they could take. The path ran beyond Groveland—their desired destination—to the southernmost point of Ohio. They approached and analyzed the latest map.

"Looks like we're about halfway there," Leo sipped the water Phoenix gave him.

"I hate to be the bearer of bad news, but it's after nine a.m. I bet President Jamen knows we've "escaped" by now."

Leo looked ahead and pointed. "Might need to call an audible. Those railroad tracks have been running parallel with the stream this whole time. Maybe we look to hop aboard some train—or at least travel up on the tracks, out of sight."

"You think we're on the television now? Wanted? Rewards out for our heads?" Autumn pondered.

"Just keep focused on the plan. You believe, you receive; you doubt, you go without," Leo quoted one of his favorite lines from the movie *Together*.

Autumn recognized that line, and she knew Leo would be thinking of his family. Before she could say anything to console him, "Oh my gosh! It's Toll!" She dangled the walkie-talkie in the air.

"Answer!" Leo came closer so he could hear.

"How are you kids holding up?" Toll spoke.

"We're all good! You?" Autumn inquired.

"Good, good. Just checking in. I have some news," Toll struggled to find his words. "You see, you both—along with the Oliver family—are on the news right now. You're all wanted fugitives of the N.U.S. with a reward out for any information leading to your whereabouts."

Autumn tried to calm the shaky nerves of the group, "We figured that."

"Oh, I know. I'm only reporting what I know to you as a courtesy. I wanted everyone to be on the same page. You'll be fine. I heard the Oliver family is working with some really smart people; people good at keeping a low profile, if you know what I'm saying," Toll said, providing more relief than he knew.

They made a plan to check in later in the day. Autumn and Leo went up to the railroad tracks, with newly found hope racing through their veins.

Chapter 31

Overgrown grasses and unmanicured shrubs sheltered the wooden tracks in a secluded area where only trains would travel. It was as if time stood still along the tracks. Each direction off the tracks was downhill, causing them to be on top of a small plateau with nowhere to go. The brutal October heat pushed beads of sweat down their foreheads.

Leo threw his bike to the ground. "I need to stop," he put his hands on his knees. "It feels weird like I'm shaking." Each time the wheels of the bike went over a track, vibrations filled their bodies.

Autumn felt the same way. Without a word, she stopped and took in her surroundings.

"Think we're getting close?" Leo managed as he took a swig of water.

"Should be."

"When are we going to get off the tracks?"

"Doesn't look like there's anywhere to go at the moment. As soon as we see an opportunity, we'll get off the tracks. As long as we're heading south, we're good, and based on the sun, we're heading in the right direction," Autumn assured.

"We are kind of vulnerable right now," Leo observed. "In the middle of nowhere, no way to escape."

"Nobody's going to find us out this way though. It's so remote. There's only a little land on each side of us. The only real way to chase us down would be someone on the tracks. We ought to be more concerned with the sun stomping down on us."

"In school, our teachers rarely tell us about the past. But, Mr. Holt—the rebel, fills us in on *some* facts. He actually sparked my interest in the area. Anyhow, he told us that Ohio had snow days—days off from school due to winter weather—in mid-April. That's crazy to me! *Now*, I mean, I can't remember the last time it wasn't at least seventy-five degrees. What's Florida like?" Leo questioned as he started walking alongside his bike, just ahead of Autumn.

"Florida used to be more like Ohio is now."

"Hot year-round?"

"Yeah, pretty much. We used to only have one hurricane season a year. Now, we're threatened year-round. The heat is too much; wildfires just start out of the blue; we face serious threats of both droughts and floods."

"Wow, that's tough," Leo empathized.

"It has also shrunk significantly. We used to be the fourth largest state in the former United States. My mom, who used to teach history, said it'd be the twenty-fifth largest state if we reunited as a nation today."

"That's wild!" Leo loved learning new information.

"That's why we need to save and change the world. This is just one state! In some places throughout the world, the heat is even contributing to the discovery of viruses from fifty thousand years ago. Catastrophe is lurking—"

Choo! Choo! A train interrupted their conversation. Black smoke entered the air as the train raced closer to them.

"What do we do?" Leo shouted.

"Come on," Autumn sprinted toward the train, pushing her bike. Leo didn't know what to do; he followed her lead.

Choo! Choo! The train sang again. The conductor saw them

on the track but could only let them know the train was coming. It'd take too long to put on the brakes.

Choo! Choo!

The train whizzed closer; one thousand feet away. They were playing chicken with a three thousand-ton piece of steel. Nine hundred feet away... eight hundred feet away...

"Trust me! Follow me!" Autumn hollered back.

Leo couldn't hear anything.

Five hundred feet away.

Autumn lifted up the front wheel of her bike. She ran off the right side of the tracks. Leo followed instinctively. The train zoomed by, barely missing them in their act of derring-do.

"That was fun, huh?" Autumn's teeth chattered as she panted, trying to get her legs to stop shaking.

"*Fun*? *Fun*? We almost got *killed*!"

"Okay, fun and lucky."

"Why'd we do that? We could've just stood by and waited!" He reminded her as he searched for his breath.

"Relax. I didn't put us at risk for no reason. Every train conductor rides with a security guard."

"So?" anger was still the dominant tone in Leo's voice.

Autumn defended her actions, "If we stood on the side of the tracks and waved at the train like a couple of children, they could've identified us. Our pictures are plastered all over thanks to President Jamen's desire to propagate his people into thinking we committed one of the worst crimes of the century."

"Now they think it's a couple of dumb kids instead of two fugitives," Leo nodded his head. "Good idea."

"They usually have cameras on the top of trains. Hopefully, they didn't get a good look at us."

The train appeared to be out of sight. Their adrenaline was

still pumping as they continued their journey along the tracks. Just as they thought they were in the clear, they heard: *Rhummm! Rhummm! Rhummm!*

Autumn squinted. "Security guard!" she shouted.

A motorcycle took off out of the caboose. It was closing in on them. Leo picked up the rocks that bedded the track. He started chucking them as far as he could, in the motorcycle's direction. Autumn did the same. There was nowhere to run; there was nowhere to hide. The security guard slowed a bit, trying their best to maneuver through the storm of stones. *Ding*. As the rider raced closer, the rocks embodied the motorcycle and hammered their helmet. Autumn jumped one way and Leo the other.

The rider came to a screeching halt, as the motorcycle became perpendicular to the railroad track. Brown, grayish dust filled the air. The driver removed their helmet. A blonde-haired security guard pointed a taser in their direction.

"Don't move!" They demanded.

Leo and Autumn made their way back onto the tracks.

"What's the problem, officer?" Leo had his hands up.

"Leo Oliver and Autumn Log, you're wanted for the destruction of property and the felonious crime of escaping federal custody." The security guard was well-informed of the situation. Silence ensued for the next fifteen seconds; the security guard barked, "Put your hands on your heads." They did just that. "I've alerted the authorities in this region. They're on their way. We are waiting right here until they arrive."

"Maybe we can work out a deal," Autumn began negotiations.

The guard shook their head.

She continued, "Being a young officer, you'll be promoted for turning us in today. This is the bust of your life. How long have you been an authority?"

"I'm a security guard for the train, not an authority officer."

"But this will help you become one, no?" Autumn knew it would.

"Yes." The security guard's inexperience leaked out.

Leo put his hands down.

"Put 'em up!" The security guard didn't give little weight to the potential peril of dealing with two wanted felons.

"My arms are tired! We're in the middle of nowhere!" Leo hollered as he walked toward the officer. "Who knows how long it'll be until they get here."

"Don't come any closer!"

"Listen, I know you're probably exhausted from working long hours, chasing the dream, trying to make a real difference on this planet. I have to ask, is the dream really hovering over people?" Leo tried to identify with them. "Look, we can bring trees back to life. Please, we need some help. We clearly know what we're doing. The world will end by the end of the year if we're stopped. We're trying to save the world. Help us! Be part of that change! Please!" Leo pleaded.

The security guard gave the idea some thought, but they eventually responded, "I'm sorry. I can't—"

Leo attacked them.

Zap! Zap!

"Ahh!" Leo shrieked; he took a tase to the right tricep. Fifty thousand volts of electricity knocked him to the side, and he involuntarily rolled down the plateau, into the tall grasses.

Autumn leapt into action; she jumped on the security guard's back and knocked the taser free. She put them in a headlock; the security guard stumbled, causing them both to timber. Autumn tried holding the headlock but they got free. They squared off as if in a boxing match. Autumn carefully approached her opponent and threw the first punch. She landed it in their arm. The security guard countered, hitting Autumn in the face with an uppercut. Remaining on her feet, Autumn threw a jab with her left hand. The fight bought enough time for Leo to come back and remove the barbs from the taser. Blood ran down his arm. He was still able to snag the taser.

"Stop it!" he managed. "Put 'em up!" Leo mocked. The security guard could only stand by as Autumn and Leo gathered their backpacks.

With no other option, Autumn stood up the motorcycle. "Hop on," she revved up the hog. The security guard watched them ride off on the stolen steel horse.

Chapter 32

They blasted up the track a few miles. Thankfully, there was an opportunity to veer off onto a main road: *State Route 43*. Based on the location of the sun, they made a split-second decision to continue to travel south. They were getting close; there were signs of abandonment and little population. For example, cardinal directions were omitted from dilapidated street signs.

Autumn pulled off behind a run-down Burger Hut. Once they cut off the motorcycle, there were no other sounds or signs of life. It was the perfect rest stop; the parking lot was deserted. It housed a forgotten-about dumpster with some wicked awesome graffiti, some tall grasses and easy access to a main road.

"Here, let me see those taser wounds," Autumn lifted his shirt to examine where the security guard hit him. "Looks like it's just on the tricep."

"Yeah, so much muscle; I'll be fine," he winked.

"Here, let me clean it out with—" Autumn was interrupted by authority officer sirens echoing in the distance.

"That's for us," Leo grimaced, gripping his right arm.

"Don't worry; we're safe," Autumn neglected to tell him her fear of infection.

"They probably have trackers in the security guard's vehicle. We have to move!"

They ditched the motorcycle and crawled through some broken fence, warily maneuvering around shards of glass. They kept low in tall grasses, trying their best to flee the scene. Even though they made it a safe distance away from the Burger Hut, they could tell authority officers were in the region; they definitely located the motorcycle by now.

"Let me see that wound," Autumn grabbed again. She took her water bottle from her backpack and poured it over Leo's bloody tricep. The cut widened; blood was seeping now. Autumn helped Leo remove his shirt completely. The once white shirt was now an array of various dark colors. Leo made his face as Autumn removed it.

His neck muscles flexed each time the water hit the wound. "How's it look?" Leo beseeched.

Autumn was hesitant, "It looks good. You'll be fine," her voice was different than usual.

"What's wrong?"

"No, nothing." It was a minor wound, but if they didn't stop the bleeding, they'd have real trouble.

"I know you better than that. I can hear it in your voice. What's wrong?"

Autumn was trying her best to disguise her tone. As it appeared, it was one of fear… but it was more than that. "You're going to be fine. We just need to find a store or something; we need to clean it out better and get it covered so there's no risk of infection." She kept working on ways to stop the bleeding.

Her response allowed Leo comfort and confidence to relax his face and practice some deep breathing.

As she worked, Autumn could no longer deny *the more than that* in her voice; not to herself, anyway. She was starting to feel feelings she never felt before. She secretly liked the opportunity to care for Leo. After taking a little more time than needed to slowly clean some of the surprisingly sculpture-like muscles around his injury, she finally wrapped his shirt around his arm as tightly as she could. "This should stop it."

"Thanks," Leo grabbed her hand.

"We have to keep moving." Autumn snuck a glance up the road. "There's something ahead," she noted.

The two walked in the tall grasses, parallel to the road, fully aware that there were authority officers sprinkled throughout the vicinity. They figured the low population ought to yield low authority officer ratios in the surrounding town.

"It looks like a strip mall ahead," Autumn noted. It would have been perfect; there was a pizza shop, health clinic, thrift shop, book store, and mini-mart… the only problem was that they were all out of business except for the mini-mart.

"Hang out over there," Autumn nodded as she rerouted toward *Mikey's Quick Stop*.

A bell let the employee in the back of the store know someone was inside the establishment. Autumn kept her head down and tried to locate some essential items like water bottles, pain medicine, maps, new shirts… anything that could help.

"Welcome to *Mikey's!*" an unconcerned voice finally shouted from the backroom storage area. "I'll be right with you."

It was an environment Autumn was unused to. Usually, she'd be watched like a hawk by someone—authority, security, employees—what have you. Not in this part of town. Autumn had her supplies in her hands and was basically loitering, searching for a bright idea on how to actually get away with them. Truth be told, she could have just exited; the employee wouldn't have been any the wiser. But she was worried about the cameras and wanted to try her best to avoid any extra suspicion. Just then, there was a *boom* from the backroom storage area. It was her chance, her cue. She darted out of the store. She saw Leo; he hurriedly waved her his way. Success was on the horizon. Just then, something intangible grabbed her consciousness: what if that person was hurt? She froze. She put the supplies on the ground, made a 180-degree turn, and went back to help the employee.

"Hello?" She announced her return.

"Hello? I'm okay but can you please come back here and give me a hand?"

Autumn entered the back room. There was someone under a large box right next to a knocked-down ladder. "My goodness," Autumn lifted the box off the person.

The person laughed, "Oh, honey! Thank you so much! These ol' legs aren't what they used to be." The person made their way to their feet while Autumn handed them their glasses that apparently went flying in the crash. "What's your name, dear?"

"Um—I'm, uh, my name is August."

"Are you serious?" they responded. "*My* name is August! Get out of town!" They held up their employee badge as proof.

Autumn couldn't believe it. "I'm trying," she responded light-heartedly even though she actually was trying to get out of town as soon as possible.

"No, no. I'm kidding. August, listen, please help get this box to the front of the store. I'm getting ready to decorate for the holidays."

"Sure," Autumn couldn't say no. She lifted the box to the store's shopping sector.

"Oh, I love it so much. I like to make a hodgepodge of enjoyment, so it takes me weeks to decorate. We don't get many visitors out this way—I'm sure you can tell—but I like being away from it all."

"I'm sure it's beautifully done."

"Ah, thanks, August. Where are you from? Maybe you can come back and see it when it's finito."

Autumn's response was delayed as she caught a glimpse of the television behind the counter. August was in their own world, oblivious. Still, sweat poured from Autumn as if she were training for the Olympics. "I actually have to get going."

"I understand. But what did you come in here for?"

Autumn's usual quick wit was acting higgledy-piggledy. She glanced at the television again. Pictures of her and Leo were plastered on the screen, along with the word: *WANTED*.

"Never mind, dear. I can tell you are a private person. But please, for helping me out, take whatever you need. No charge. Honest. It was nice meeting you," August shook Autumn's hand.

"Thank you so much," Autumn modestly grabbed two water bottles, trying not to reveal her anxiety. "Good luck with the decorations." She snagged one more glance at the television; the list paraded their rap sheet:

Autumn Log and Leo Oliver are WANTED!
- *Attempted Murder of a Security Guard,*
- *Robbery – Authority Vehicle*
- *Destruction of a Hospital and Restaurant*
- *Escaping Prison*
- *Causing Natural Disaster*
- *Public Endangerment*

Autumn composed herself enough to exit, grab the supplies and make her way back to Leo.

"Took you long enough," Leo looked at her confused. "What happened? I saw you go back inside."

"Just trying to be a good person. It paid off for us, but we have to get moving. Now! Take these; they're the only pain meds I could get my hands on."

Leo swigged down two pain tablets. He made his way to his feet with Autumn's assistance, as he was trying not to use his tased arm at all.

"They're saying we nearly killed that security guard."

"What do you mean?" Leo worried.

"They're running news ads with our pictures. Luckily the worker didn't pay any attention to it."

"We didn't almost kill them," Leo objected.

"They made it look like we killed people because of our damage to the hospital too. No patients were injured! They're lying!" Autumn knew there'd be propaganda but never envisioned it to this extreme. "They said we caused natural disaster! They know nothing!"

"We have to call Alder and Toll. Check in with them to see what's going on."

Autumn hit the call button on the blue walkie-talkie they gave them. "Toll? Toll? Come in!"

"Well, well, well, if it isn't Bonnie and Clyde," a familiar voice replied. It wasn't Alder. Or Toll.

"Who is this?"

"Young lady, you're in a lot of trouble. So are you and your friends. Toll and Mr. Mayor here are in big trouble. I'm thinking a life sentence in prison ought to do. Caught them red-handed. You'll never believe it; these yahoos were trying to regrow a tree." President Jamen laughed diabolically.

"They had nothing to do with it, leave them alone. Please!" Autumn begged.

"At least *I* know how to regrow trees, now. Just like you two whippersnappers. A valuable skill for the president of the New United States, don't ya' think? The re-election is in the bag now. I'm a magician too; tomfoolery if I don't make it six terms in a row come November."

"Mr. President, trees are vital to the survival of the country. You know in your heart we need them," Autumn professed.

"We don't," he responded convincingly. "I won't regrow any trees, and tell your partner that his family is going to be... chopped down... at Central Park," he snickered at his play on words.

Leo heard everything and grabbed the walkie-talkie. "We're just getting started." He chucked the walkie-talkie into the distance. "Let's go," he commanded, holding his arm, trying to prevent the bleeding.

They broke off into a jog, now racing against the night sky, which painted a darker shade by the minute. They maneuvered their way to the side of the road, hoping the illumination from sparing street lights could provide some guidance. The road was abandoned. Gray, rocky gravel kicked up behind them when they jogged. At times, the bottoms of their shoes lost traction and they would glide over parts of the gravel nearly losing their balance. Traveling was strenuous but proved more secure as the moon took center stage.

There weren't many places along the way to stop. They passed a *Midnight Motel*, a four-nozzle gas station, and an abandoned bar with metal bars in the windows. They were in the middle of nowhere.

They jogged for as long as they could and walked when they were tired. Leo's watch made his wrist uncomfortable and sticky from the sweat. His eyes were drawn to that watch like a moth to light. The black band and silver rectangle face served as a reminder that they were against time. They needed to spring this plan into action to save as many people as they could, including their families.

Chapter 33

The pair traveled all night. The moon took a bow and gave way to the sun, which peaked up over the horizon. Their tired eyes spotted an open field in the distance, surrounded with tall grasses. They plopped down like a person in a recliner that ate too much. Some much-needed relaxation was pleasantly interrupted by a delicious aroma wave that rode its way into their nostrils.

"Where's that coming from?" Autumn sat up at the first sign of civilization in quite some time. The nearby road appeared to curve around two brownish-red, old barns that sat alongside the road.

"Finally, some life," Leo took a deep breath to gain strength to keep going.

"We have to be careful. We don't know who lives there. They might be fixing to turn us in; remember, Toll warned us about locals."

They followed the curve in the road, walking on eggshells, keeping their heads on a swivel. "A doughnut shop!" Leo exclaimed.

"What?" Autumn couldn't believe it.

It was the last thing they expected to be around the road's bend. *D's Doughnuts* housed a five-car parking lot. The orange sign had the word *OPEN* written in capital letters but it was just as deserted as every other business they crossed along their journey.

"I hope they have custard filling," Leo nearly drooled as he pulled the door open for Autumn.

"Let's be quick," she whispered.

"We're fine. We need to eat something." Nobody was there to take their order. Only soft, older music echoed off the walls. "Let's just go," Leo said disappointedly. "Nobody's here."

"No, you're right; we have to eat something. You've lost too much blood. We need to fill up our water bottles and get some rest."

Leo leaned over the counter, and he peered through the machinery but saw nothing. "Let's go around back."

They walked by the steel machines and into the back of the kitchen. There was an old screen door, barely hanging by its hinges, with a faded-red wooden base. Outside, a man was working on something at a picnic table; something with his hands. He appeared to be a bit older. He had gray hair; he squinted up through his glasses; his hands were shaking, and he didn't even hear Autumn and Leo.

"Excuse me, sir," Leo began. The man didn't respond. He tried clearing his throat, "Excuse me, sir."

Nothing. They slowly approached him, not wanting to scare him. They were tigers in the wild, approaching their prey with no intention of pouncing. Autumn tapped his shoulder.

The man, startled, looked back at them and grabbed his chest. Autumn and Leo simultaneously lifted their hands in the air and took a few steps back to show they meant no harm. Once he realized this, he took a few deep breaths and began to chuckle.

"You kids scared me!" His smile was so contagious that Autumn and Leo couldn't help but smile back.

"Sorry about that, sir," Leo started. "We were interested in some doughnuts. We didn't mean to bother you; we have come a long way and are starving."

"Yes, yes," the old man tried his best to stand. He reached for his black cane. He was excited to finally have some company. "I don't get customers too often. Usually just people who take the back way to Groveland to do some camping. It sure is refreshing to see some youth in the neighborhood."

"Groveland is close by?" Autumn inquired nonchalantly.

"Yes, dear. Hug the road and you'll find the office. They'll set you up real nice," D led them back inside the shop. "I'm D, and this is my property; technically it's on Groveland grounds."

"Thanks," Autumn glanced at Leo. They couldn't help but share a smile knowing they were close.

"What'll it be?" D was ready for their order.

"May I please have a custard, glazed, and pink frosting with the sprinkles?" Leo ordered a mouthful of choices.

"Of course. And for the lady?"

"I'll have a Boston Cream and strawberry, please."

Leo went to pretend to pull out his wallet, "How much, sir?"

"On the house; don't you worry about that," D insisted.

"Are you sure?" Autumn asked for some reason. They had no money but figured it was still decent to offer.

"Just let an old man have a doughnut with you," D proposed.

"Boss won't be mad?" Leo bantered.

"Boss passed away a few years ago. She was pretty great. Kept me in line," D showed love to his late wife. "Yep, we started this back with my great-great-grandfather. My name is D Nseert the third, but all my friends call me D. Place has been in the family for generations."

Autumn and Leo took a booth with D. There were other tables spaced out around the old-diner-looking place, plenty of room if he drew the customers.

"Yes, time sure does stand still around these parts," D

noticed them canvasing his establishment.

"This place is awesome!" Leo pointed out.

"Nothing like a good doughnut to brighten your day," D's energy was so uplifting. You couldn't help but be positive when you were around him.

"You've been here to see Groveland get built up over the last few decades, then?" Autumn assumed.

D seemed taken aback by her question, "Yes! What interests you in Groveland?"

"Just curious is all. I've heard stories from my folks," Autumn was growing into a great liar.

"Yes, they have fairly newer cabins. No trees surrounding it anymore. That was the fun of it—my granddaddy always used to tell us they'd sway from tree swings and splash into the river."

"Did they use those trees to make the cabins?" Leo gently pried.

"Why, I believe so," D paused. "Now, are you two planning on regrowing some trees in the area?"

Chapter 34

Autumn flung from the orange-leather booth.

"Take it easy," D extended his hand to Leo's. "I would've already phoned the authorities if I was gonna' turn you kids in. I've been watching the news. I may be old but I'm still pretty sharp. Your pictures are everywhere. Have you really been up to all that nonsense?"

"Parts of it are true," Leo admitted.

"What parts?" D queried.

Autumn cut in, "Look, if your family has been in the area for quite some time, you'd know who Dr. Rea Log was."

"Ah, yes! Mad scientist many moons ago. He and his friends came up with an idea of how to regrow trees," D was familiar.

Autumn's eyes widened.

"Wow," Leo blurted, "I've never seen her speechless. Maybe they should call you Dr. D."

Autumn pretended to snicker at him. The guys smiled.

"I want to see how it's done!" D started his long process of getting out of his seat.

"We're in a hurry, we don't really have time," Autumn tried to play it off. "We should get going though, we have an ambitious agenda."

"I can help," D offered.

"Why help? Why not turn us in for millions?" Leo wondered in all seriousness.

"My family is on your side. This land is our land. It has been for years. We didn't want the trees to go. We know we need them to survive. In all our time, no one had the courage or the skills to make any real changes. You two are doing just that."

"We're trying. It's a lot harder than you think," Autumn admitted.

"Look, I may be lonely but my family's love for the land still gives me hope. I can't leave it. I helped build those cabins. Plus, I've been tracking cabin rentals from my lookout," D got up and led them outside the doughnut shop to the edge of the road. The beautiful view provided a top-down picture of the wide-open landscape that had cabins plopped down every so often.

"You built those cabins?" Autumn reached to check her phone for the materials list.

"Sure did. Well, six of them anyway. We cut down the trees and would work right there," D explained.

"In order to regrow the trees, we need to know what material came from exactly what stump," Leo explained.

D nodded. "You should have everything you need down there. We didn't have the most resources, so we had to be innovative. No trucks were used to haul anything."

Autumn skimmed the materials list. "I have their location."

"Yep, should be government record. We had to report our every move, even back then. I know for a fact we used lover trees and black oaks. Those were my wife's favorites. Broke my heart to chop them down, but I knew people would enjoy the cabins, the land, the experience… life."

"Lover trees?" Autumn was curious.

"You'll see," D nodded his head. "Listen, due to security making their rounds, we won't have much time to regrow," D was afraid they wouldn't tackle all that they had planned.

"One is better than none," Leo was optimistic.

"I have some tools in the shed. Saws, blades. Take whatever you'll need," D offered his place for the kids to work, ensuring nobody would stop by. Even better, he used his telescope to scope out what cabins were occupied. According to D's calculations, Cabins 1, 2, 3 and 5 were vacant. Only Cabins 4 and 6 had renters. Starting at Cabin 1 was most logical because not only did it create the greatest distance between the other campers, it also provided the quickest escape route.

Seamlessly, for the next few hours, they crossed their *t's* and dotted their *i's*. It was a great opportunity to plan and catch their breath following their physically demanding trip.

D allowed them the chance to turn on the boob tube and learn what lies the president was spreading—with the media's help. *Breaking News* scrolled across the bottom of the television screen while reporters sat in a semi-circle desk-like format debating the situation.

The *Breaking News* read:

President Jamen declares more trees are being regrown at an alarming rate. Autumn Log and Leo Oliver have accomplices; three have been captured. Anyone who tries to help them will earn life sentences in prison. The reward for them is $100 million... dead or alive.

"Phoenix," Leo blurted. "He's the third. The other two are Toll and Alder."

"*Dead or alive?*" Autumn stressed, "How can adults be so deceiving and manipulative toward harming people, especially the young?" Her hands flew in the air, propelled by frustration.

D quickly clicked off the boob tube. "Hey, I never told you about my wife..." D strategically intervened, coming between the teens and the endless worries floating in their imaginations. He paused for the perfect amount of time which prompted the question to not be rhetorical. He forced Autumn's play.

"No, D. You haven't," she obliged.

"Well, my bride, Ivry, was magic. You would've loved her, I swear of it," D's genuineness took over. "When they were cutting down the last of the trees in Groveland, and I was helping build the cabins, she stood in solidarity with a small group of people. She faced bulldozers and local authority officers square in the face, fearless. You know why?" D tried to draw the kids into the message he was trying to deliver.

"Why?" Leo obliged this time.

"She knew her identity. She knew where she stood. She could then act. She could worry about her *feelings* later. We can always worry later. Now's not the time to overthink, worry, or feel. You have already proven you can do hard things," D encouraged. "It's time to act!"

Autumn agreed. "My father always says: *can't get today back.*"

Leo nodded his head. "Yes, we are going to get this done. For everyone."

"That's the spirit," D's eyes sparkled. "Ivry would be proud, I know it. Even though the trees are gone, she made real change here. She sparked the movement to build locally to help prevent transportation, which would have contributed to the pollution problem; she kept jobs local as well; she even preserved some of the rivers that run through here. The only thing she loved more than the land was forcing guests to leave us with a full belly." This made Autumn and Leo smile. "She'd have all kinds of food down your throat by now. Oh, oh…" he trailed off in a panic, "It's dinner time; I have to feed you," he huffed and puffed like an old car starting up, motoring toward preparing some much-needed nourishment.

The three of them helped prepare a modest meal. In the process, the three chatted, took a brain break and allowed themselves to be human. That included taking in the Crayola Sky Blue backdrop as the sun set picturesquely behind the mountains of Groveland. Laughter accompanied stories of the past into the evening. In D's mind: mission accomplished.

"Well, it's quitting time for me," D and his cane shakily made their way to his home adjacent to the doughnut shop. "You kiddos need your rest. There's lots of dips and turns along the way to the cabins that you'll have to be on the lookout for come go time. This land used to be full of life… not so much anymore. I hope trees can bring that life back. Family, friends and love are the future… I know it." He disappeared into his yellow painted—although chipped in many areas—perfect home for him.

Leo and Autumn let the fire they started continue to burn as they got comfortable under the stars. Their view went on forever; it was like they were on the upper end of an ice cream cone, and it narrowed as they looked down into the land. They could see bonfires—other campers doing the same thing they were doing. The good news: there were no bonfires outside the cabins D presumed vacant.

"That's the star again. My favorite," Leo pointed.

"I know, the moon and the two that look like they make a half-circle. I think you mumbled something about it at Kant State," she tried to play it cool, realizing the comment revealed feelings.

Leo smiled and snuck his arm around Autumn. She nestled in. The awkward silence was painful. It was a necessary pain, though. Their insides were butterfly sanctuaries; it was a miracle they didn't lift off into the air and fly away.

"Let me know if your arm starts to fall asleep," Autumn

cooed. "I hate the tingly movements that paralyze my arm when it happens."

"Okay. I will let you know," Leo lied. His skin tightened: goosebumps. It felt like every hair on his body was standing straight up, magnetized by something in the sky.

Autumn didn't know what to do with her hands; she tried to play it cool but honestly just felt like a worm. Her head was the only part of her body that was touching Leo's. She became more and more uncomfortable from the strain on her neck, but would never admit it.

Leo focused on his breathing. He hoped she couldn't tell that his heart was beating faster than an angry drummer at band practice. Actually, there was no disguising it, so the real hope rested on her not mentioning it, making him feel silly.

Out of the beautiful black sky, a shooting star brightened up the landscape. It shot across so fast and so smooth. It looked like the end of the star would never catch the front of the star. It happened in a blink; then, it disappeared.

"Whoa, did you see that?" Leo sat up; he would've jumped up like a rocket if Autumn wasn't lying on his chest.

"Yep. Amazing," Autumn's blasé response proved she'd seen way more shooting stars than Leo. Sleeping outdoors was becoming a norm for her. "Make a wish!"

"A wish?"

"Yep. I don't know if it works, but it gives me hope. Hope that I need when I'm out here all alone," Autumn hesitated to reveal her true self. "You probably think I'm a weirdo… someone who wishes on stars."

"I don't think that at all. Plus, even if I did, who would I tell? And if I did tell, well, the world will be over soon," he joked. Autumn gently slapped him, and her hand found a home over his heart. "I'm kidding; we're going to save it." Leo, still not realizing how they fell into each other, whispered, "Plus, you're not all alone anymore."

Autumn turned her head and lifted her body up ever so slightly so their lips could be close by. Her eyes locked with his; then their smiles. Their smiles met halfway; their eyes closed; and they shared a magical, awkward, I-hope-this-person-kisses-me-back, first few kisses. Unsure how the other felt, they each quickly snuck a peek to see what the other person was doing, only to catch one another looking.

"Wow, that wish thing *does* work," Leo teased then leaned in for more.

Another shooting star took center stage. Autumn kissed him one more time and reminded him to make another wish as she laid her head back down on his chest, allowing the moon to be their nightlight.

Chapter 35

Badoom. Badoom. Badoom. Leo's heart skipped a beat with every passing ring that nobody answered. He borrowed D's landline in the doughnut shop to try touch base with his family before breakfast. He figured using a landline would make it more challenging to trace the call. He was worried, given the fact President Jamen mentioned Central Park. *Badoom. Badoom. Badoom.* He took a deep breath and held it in his cheeks, making his face look like it was stuffed with marshmallows, then exhaled slowly. His leg shook faster than lightning. *Why was nobody answering? Had they been caught? Would this call tip off the authorities regarding their whereabouts?* Anxiety was on the loose inside of his mind. *Badoom. Badoom. Badoom.*

Finally: "Hello?"

"Uncle Cliff! It's Leo."

"Hey, Leo!" his uncle said enthusiastically.

"How's everything? Is my family still all good? No visits from the President?"

"Not yet, anyway. We're all fine. Here, I'll put your mother on the line." Uncle Cliff handed the phone to Rosie.

"Leo, honey, how are you?" Rosie sounded frantic but was trying to make the most of the situation.

"Good, we're fine," an overwhelming feeling of relief flooded his soul. "We made some friends along the way that have been helping us. We're wanted fugitives though."

"I see that. We're wanted too. It seems the only time these

nations want to work together is to stop change from occurring," Rosie griped.

"Are you guys doing all right? It's so nice to… just… hear your voice."

"We've started regrowing in Central Park. Your father and brother have been posing as unhoused people for the last few nights. The authorities here can't figure out who or what is causing trees to regrow. We've regrown at least a dozen."

"Good! Have you heard from them recently?"

"Two days ago," there was silence. "They're fine. Don't worry. They're worried about *you*." Rosie paused briefly and added, "Your sister and cousin—the nerds that they are, tapped into the authorities' communication system. It sounds like they're debating letting the public know the extent and reasoning of our work—most likely due to fear of inspiring others to help, or to avoid making themselves look silly."

"We met President Jamen. He's going to make sure he finds us. He already captured Toll and Alder," Leo informed.

"I know."

"That made news too?"

"Sweetie, brace yourself," Rosie started. "They were both sentenced to life in prison… they made it a nationally televised event in the N.U.S. and New North. They were even beaten. Their families had to watch."

"*What*? That's barbaric!"

"We couldn't believe it either. They're trying to paint *us* as the villains; and if you help *us*, you'll be prosecuted to the fullest extent of the law. Leo, this is way bigger than we thought. This is about the environment, Earth, and life. For us, home no longer exists. If we save the world, they'll say it was never going to end. If we don't save the world, well, then, well, we've created a lose-

lose situation," Rosie finally found her wording.

Leo didn't say anything for a few seconds.

Rosie knew his guilt was growing. "Don't let your beautiful mind think we had any other choice. Your father and I heard the rumors for decades. We always wanted to take action. When I first met your dad there was *nothing* we couldn't do."

"Oh yeah?"

"We protested high gas prices and cameras being put up in private locations," she chuckled. "One time your father and I stood outside protesting the destruction of land when it was pouring rain. Every person stayed. Your father could persuade people to eat a ketchup popsicle while wearing white gloves. He was good. We were a good team. So good, that the authorities saw us as a threat. I bet you didn't know that about your old folks."

"No you weren't!" Leo couldn't believe it.

"Swear. They offered us our current jobs. We couldn't refuse at the time. At first, they led us to believe we would be working for the good of the people. In fact, it started out that way. We got married, thought we were changing the world, then had you guys. Just about the time you were born, we found out that people at our workplace were manipulating us. I think they offered us the jobs in exchange for not *rocking the boat.*"

"What'd you do?"

"We found out when we identified the places around us that needed things like food and cleaner water, they took that information and built new business buildings over the land. It forced people to move all over the country. Now it doesn't look like there is a struggling area in the N.U.S. It was all done in order to provide the illusion we were the most powerful country in the world," she implied that was the goal at the time.

"Why didn't you try to fight to stop it?"

"We were threatened. They said we'd lose our jobs, healthcare, and income; our names would be dragged through the mud. We had to adapt. We did what we had to in order to survive. We jumped through hoops to save you and our family," there was a pause. "And here we are today. We've wanted to rebel for quite some time. We just thought it was impossible. Turns out we just needed you, your siblings, and Autumn to show us what courage looked like," Rosie praised.

"Thanks, Mom; *you guys* are the brave ones."

Rosie fought back tears knowing this could be the last time she talked to her oldest son, "You go out and regrow as many trees as you can. We don't quit."

Leo could sense it, "Okay, we will. And we're coming to New York next."

"Don't! We will be on the move. We're leaving as soon as your father and brother get back. They're sure to find us any day now."

"How will we know when to meet up?" Leo already knew there was no answer but asked anyway.

"I don't know, dear."

"I love you," Leo knew they would be lucky to see each other again.

"Love you more."

"Love you more, Mom. Tell everyone I love them," Leo hung up the phone.

Leo joined D and Autumn for breakfast.

"Well, it's about half past seven. I reckon you kids hit the road," D announced. D handed them bottled water and food bars for their mission. "Here are a couple of my finest tools," D also handed them two axes, recently sharpened.

"Thanks, D!" Leo couldn't find any other words; he could only look at D.

Nobody could find the words or the courage to say anything else. Mutual respect and saying goodbye have that effect. They only nodded to each other, and Autumn and Leo went on their way.

Chapter 36

"This is going to happen fast. Two miles downhill then we start regrowing," Autumn clarified.

They both had a little extra pep in their steps. They didn't stop once; they didn't speak once; they carefully and slowly balanced themselves down the rocky soil. They headed east, toward Cabin 1. Cabin 1 was unoccupied and gave them the best chance to get a head start on an escape route.

The "woods" were empty. Large rocks, tall grasses and an unkept landscape provided at least some level of inconspicuousness. It was a Monday afternoon, now the first day of November. Most people were working or at school. The wind picked up a bit as Cabin 1 became visible.

Once they arrived, Autumn threw down her backpack and examined the area. Leo was already in his bag, pulling out the tools D gave him. The two moved together in perfect harmony, making decisions based on a balanced diet of D's advice and the intel Autumn had on the jump drive. They located the stumps and conversed about the materials used in each. They meticulously disassembled the cabin piece by piece, either with force or the axes D provided. They were cognizant of the noise and their surroundings, aiming to draw zero attention to the life-size puzzle they were assembling.

Leo worked on pulling the stairs apart. Autumn focused on the handrail angled down the cabin stairs. She shook the wood free of the nails. D's advice ran through their heads like kids

playing tag on the playground:
- *Place the steps and handrail on the correct stump.*
- *Axe down the supports that held the cabin up.*
- *Place all that wood on another stump.*

They were set to regrow two trees easier than anticipated. Adhering to the plan, they held off until all of the stumps were ready for a rapid regrow session. The last thing they wanted to do was pull the tarp and draw premature attention to their mission.

"This is going to be much harder now," Autumn recognized. "These cabins are a good size." It was time to interact with the much larger chunks of the cabin. Like case study researchers, the pair hopped back and forth between D's advice and the intel on the jump drive.

- *Disassemble one side of the cabin.*
- *Then the other side.*
- *Then the roof.*
- *Then the floor.*
- *Try to leave them in large pieces.*
- *The trees will all be different sizes.*
- *You might have to move pieces to different stumps just in case the calculations were wrong.*

The sun started to play a factor in their efforts. Suddenly, its beauty from the morning rise was forgotten by the beating it was giving them at the moment. Over an hour went by. The likelihood of them being caught grew larger and more real by the second. No trees could block the sun; nothing was really preventing them from being seen by hikers or authority officers. Their mental toughness needed to be top-notch as stress and anxiety bubbled in their bellies.

"We're good," Autumn sensed a storm of freezing up and

fleeing might be brewing—in most people's logical thoughts, anyway.

"I know," Leo tried to *will* the desired outcome to life. Still, he made his face; the ease of having the first two trees ready to go was only an illusion of how the rest of the process was playing out.

In spite of that, they persevered. They kept going until their first draft for *materials-on-stumps* was ready for Cabin 1. All the materials were in at least a holding place, resting on potential stumps they belonged to; the wood from the entire cabin was separated into piles on five different stumps. Tarps covered them. Leo and Autumn locked eyes, nodded and pulled at the same time.

A sea of debris scattered shards of wood, tools and building materials in all directions as if it were a scene of war; Leo and Autumn ducked for cover. A cloud of dust rose, revealing two huge trees. They had the materials perfectly placed.

Leo jumped effervescently. The scene brought on evocative images, signaling a job well done and one that was worth the risk. Leo imitated one of the tree's physical makeup, which looked as if someone strong was flexing their muscles; its branches came out to a near-perfect 90-degree angle and then shot straight up again. The leaves had a yellowish, reddish appearance… again, taking on the current season.

"I can't believe how *gorgeous* they are," Leo's energy was vibrant.

The second tree was equally as large: at least eighty feet tall, king-sized… resplendent both in nature and in its leaves; a sublime portrait was painted by a greater good.

The admiration period was cut short. "We have to move!" Autumn demanded. They raced to cover the other stumps. Once one was covered, they locked eyes again and together stripped the stump of the tarp.

Another worked. It was a small tree, no larger than fifteen feet. The circumference of the bark was *maybe* three feet. The teens scurried to reorganize the final two stumps. Based on the size of the materials, they hypothesized one of them would be as huge as the two king-sized trees, and the other, much smaller.

As they were shuffling around materials, Leo made his face, struggling to find the courage to proceed as the anxieties crept out of their cave again. Autumn kept moving. "Just act!" she shouted.

He tried. He noticed one of the boards had half of a heart carved into it. He picked it up, walked over to the other stump, and sure enough, the other half of the heart was carved into a similar board. "Got it!" he proclaimed and launched it onto the pile.

Click! "Don't move!" a man loaded a gun and hollered at the two just as they were about to pull the tarps. "You, this way," he indicated through nonverbals that he wanted Leo to isolate himself away from the tree.

It was a person hunting the area with their son. The kid couldn't have been more than nine years old. Leo put his hands up and moved ever so cautiously to the directed spot.

"Please, sir," Autumn pleaded.

"Stop! Enough! I've seen the news," the man barked back. "Lanzo, these are the people I was warning you about."

"Lanzo, we're just trying to do the right thing," Leo tried to calm down the petrified kid.

"Don't you talk to my son!" the man snarled; he was foaming at the mouth, ready to be a killer, millionaire or... both.

"Okay," Autumn soothed, drawing Leo's eyes. "Call the

authorities. We're prepared to surrender peacefully. You'll get your money," she faked a smile.

The man pulled out his phone and dialed. Sirens filled the air immediately; the gigantic trees would serve as a decent GPS for the authorities.

Leo nodded. Autumn yanked the tarp just as the man said, "Hi, I'd like to report—" and he was cut off as the tree darted toward the sky. The sea of debris appeared again and sent the scenario into a frenzy. One of the branches lunged outward, cupping the man with the gun, and lifting him seventy feet in the air. He hung on for dear life; the gun was cast into the grasses as if insignificant.

Another branch punched Leo on its way up, launching him in the distance. He struggled to regain his footing; the wind was knocked out of him. While he waddled around, finding his breath, Autumn ran to the other tree and regrew it. It *was* smaller, just as they predicted; yet, compelling nonetheless: both smaller trees wound the parts of their branches around one another. It appeared as if they were holding hands.

She ran toward Lanzo. "Hey, bud. Look, we're just trying to save the planet. See those? Those are trees. *Lover trees*. Like my friend, D, told me about." She patted him on the head, then proceeded to assist Leo. "Your dad is going to be fine," Autumn reassured as Lanzo's dad was hollering, even though he was safely seated on a secure branch.

Once she made her way to Leo, they were full of bliss. They did it. Five trees in total. They looked up from where they were. *D's Doughnuts* sat atop the hill. Euphoria permeated their reality.

Chapter 37

"Freeze!" Euphoria expired. Authorities shot out circumjacently from all directions. As they say, they had them surrounded. Leo put his hands on his knees, gasping for air, making his face. Autumn raised her hands, ironically surrendering peacefully—as promised.

"What is that man doing up there?" one authority officer asked rhetorically, afraid he'd draw the short straw in aiding in his rescue. The guy was screaming for help, hugging the tree's branch, frightened for his life.

Four all-white *Groveland* authority cars with red and green writing along the sides boxed in the wanted fugitives. Although the teens were clearly outmatched, eight officers still deemed it necessary to point eight guns at the teenagers. Tension soon ballooned; all they could do was hope they wouldn't shoot. Inexperience was on full display, and when nobody acts, anyone could act. The uncomfortable silence was finally interrupted when one of the officers received a walkie-talkie call from inside the car.

They answered, "Yes, sir. Got 'em." They waited for a reply and replied back with, "Roger." They looked at their fellow officers and nodded toward Leo and Autumn. "Looks like we're not shooting today, team. The president would love to see them." They cuffed the two and put them in the back of separate cars.

The jail wasn't far away. Groveland was not close to a major city; they had their own jail, albeit only one cell. The town was clearly run down and didn't see much action.

"No matter what happens—" Autumn whispered but was rudely interrupted.

"Quiet in there! No talking! The president will be here shortly," the lead authority officer barked. When the officers weren't looking, they did their best to mouth each other words.

Leo squinted and thought Autumn mouthed, *No matter what, stay strong*.

"No mouthing words!" the same officer squashed the lip-reading efforts.

The only audible sounds in the sorry excuse for a jail were:

1. Each tick of the clock as it echoed, and

2. the swaying of a ceiling fan, whose fate hung in the balance as it wobbled like a belly dancer.

Two hours went by—no activity. Finally, suits stormed through the doors. The president darted from behind them. "Do we have an interrogation room?" he didn't even look toward the cell.

The lead officer showed him the way.

"This is it?" President Jamen looked disgusted as he tossed *The Break Room* sign off the door. Four chairs surrounded a table full of playing cards. "Bring me the girl first," he ordered as he swiped all the cards onto the floor.

Autumn fell into Leo and grabbed his hands, resisting. He held onto her hand and shook his head, but the officers pushed and shoved her out of the cell. For added personal pleasure, they threw Leo to the dusty floor. Before standing up again, he pocketed the jump drive Autumn snuck to him.

Autumn entered the makeshift interrogation room, and the president pulled out a chair for her. "Everyone else can leave." He watched the door close. "I'm done messing around!" he yelled and slammed the table. "You're *lucky* I didn't have you *killed*. All I need to know is how to cut them down. They seem unbreakable. If you tell me, I will allow you to return to Florida, unharmed."

Autumn grinned. "They can't be cut down once reassembled."

"What do you mean?"

"They. Can't. Be. Cut. *Down*," she berated condescendingly in a slower fashion. "My great-great-great-great grandfather never figured out how and neither can I."

"This is unfortunate. Mostly for you."

"Why? Think about it, you already got your use out of them. What's the harm? It sounds like a pretty smart idea to me. Use the tree for materials and when you don't need them anymore, regrow the tree."

"We didn't need the hospital?"

"Nobody ever used that wing!"

"The restaurant?"

"There are hundreds around!"

"It's a matter of principle!" the president's black hair flopped a bit and his face became a darker shade of red every tenth of a second. "People know they are illegal! We can't stop it! It looks like I can't lead!"

"All about you… typical."

"Some scientists believe they harm the planet!"

Autumn wasn't buying his lies, "The world will end in two months. Those scientists were paid to spread that rumor by greedy businessmen who only wanted materials for money and land for oil drilling. I have proof in my grandfather's journal."

"How do you know *he's* not lying?"

"Everything he said is true! The world's climate is

drastically different than years before. The weather's severity is growing at an alarming rate. Human population is increasing, and *our* land is shrinking because of these changes. People have nowhere to live! People are getting sick! There is limited clean air and water."

"You think you have this all figured out, huh?"

Autumn nagged, "Treacherous and dangerous storm patterns are wreaking havoc on the world. Life-threatening floods and natural disasters need to be addressed—or at least recognized as such."

"Look, I know that Leo's family is in New York. I'm sure yours is all over. Trees are regrowing all around North America. I've spoken with other presidents, and we agree it has to be stopped. Tell me where Leo's family is heading next; I'll let you and your family live."

"You know we're doing the right thing. Just get on board with us," Autumn pleaded, trying to persuade him.

"I *do not* agree with you!"

"Why are you talking to other presidents for the first time ever? Why are you in Groveland worried about teenagers? You're *scared*. You're *scared* we're right and you don't know how to stop us."

He walked over to the door, "Obviously you do not understand the severity of the situation." He opened the door and ordered the officer to take her back to the cell and bring in Leo who was listening to their conversation through the paper-thin walls.

"Hello, Leo," President Jamen was playing "good cop" with him. He even shook his hand. Leo was dumbfounded by this treatment. He let out a large breath of relief and a half-hearted smile. He took a seat and the president sat across from him. Leo's hands still cuffed, and wrists now bleeding from them being so tight, used his shoulder to itch his nose.

"This has gone on long enough. Look at yourself. You're bleeding, tired, hungry. You're basically an orphan now. Speaking of orphans," the president didn't let Leo's mind pause at all, "that's what you are going to be if you don't help me cut down these regrown trees. I have officers on the way to your Uncle Cliff's address in New York: 15356 Longvale Rd. If the trees aren't down immediately, I'll murder every single member of your family."

"Sir, please don't! You need to understand that the reason this is such a powerful movement is that we're unsure how to take them down. All we know is we need one thousand trees up by December or the world will literally destroy. Destroy, not in a few decades or years, but within days. Please, sir!"

"I'm not concerned with a hypothesis that has been around forever and that we will never see to be true. I need to keep *order* in this country. I *need* those trees down!" He slammed his fists on the table.

"I can't, sir!" Leo implored. "We don't know how! I'll do anything! Please don't hurt my family! I will stop regrowing them; I will stop Autumn; I will work for you to repay you! Please."

"Here's the deal," he showed him a screenshot on his phone. It was Ashton and Lewis in Central Park. "I'm going to allow you to go free."

"What?" Leo's response was incredulous.

"Yep. Go free. Walk out those doors right now."

"What about Autumn?"

"There are now two hundred fifty trees regrown in the New United States. Some guy in Kant is regrowing them; I can't believe I have to jail him for life now, just like Toll and Alder. On top of that, people over in the New North, especially in New York—at Central Park—are regrowing them. I need it to stop. If you can't remove the trees, keep them from popping up. If there are ever two hundred seventy-five trees in the New United States, I *will* kill Autumn Log. I *will* let her go next December if no other trees are regrown. That's just over a year in prison; the perfect amount of time for her to reflect on the severity of the crimes you two committed."

"You think prison is going to change her?"

"It's a special one... at the White House," he smirked sinisterly.

"Why are you doing this?" Leo couldn't grasp the reasoning for the offer.

"Why are *you* doing this? I will prove to you the world will *not* end when the new year comes."

"She'll really be free?"

"Free as a bird. And let's be honest, do you really have a choice? This is the only way you two are surviving the day."

Leo raised his hands; an officer uncuffed him and he walked out of the room. Autumn stood up to welcome him back to the cell; he didn't look at her. Instead, she looked on, perplexed, as Leo walked out of the Groveland jail, untouched.

Chapter 38

Completely up a creek without a paddle, Leo raced to the nearby tall grasses. There was a thin river that looked like it ran downstream. He splashed his face with the cold, murky water. Car door slamming drew back his attention. President Jamen wasted no time. A black SUV with the license plate, *PREZ JMN*, sped off, kicking rocks and leaving a path of dust on its way back to D.C.

Laughter in the distance drew Leo's attention to the Groveland community campsite. Families were laughing, playing games and roasting marshmallows over smaller bonfires. He recognized a tune a father was playing on an acoustic guitar. It was a sing-along he remembered as a kid. He yearned to return to his normal life; he would love to hit the studio. His greatest stresses about college, the future—it all seemed so much better than what he faced now. In the darkest of times, he tried to focus on his *why*: his family, Autumn, and oh yeah, the world.

Leo cut his pity party short. Instead of wallowing in self-deprecation, he decided to take Autumn's advice: act. He crept down like a jaguar hunting its prey and struck when nobody was looking. He was able to snag water and someone's bicycle. He peddled away from the campsite; his destination was *D's Doughnuts*.

There was a path that appeared to lead straight up to the chimney smoke he saw. The rocky hills and steep slope literally were a pain in his butt. He put his head between his legs to rest for a moment before making his final stretch toward D. As he neared, his stomach did somersaults; he wasn't sure if his mind was playing tricks on him; something smelled like it had been set ablaze.

He sprinted to check on D. The barn in the back was on fire. Flames encompassed the old shack.

"D!" he screamed in terror. No response. He ran inside the doughnut shop. No sign of him. He raced back to where he said he'd be watching them regrow trees—the outlook. To his surprise, he saw D sitting in his lawn chair, overlooking Groveland. "D! You made me worried sick!" D didn't respond. Something was wrong. He hustled over to him and to his dismay, D's eyes were closed; he was dead.

Leo jumped back, horrified. Shock took over his body as tears streamed down his cheeks. An uncontrollable shaking caused him to stumble away and hurl.

Thud! A large piece of the barn crashed, reminding him to move. Sirens sang in the distance. He wiped his mouth and ran back inside the doughnut shop. He frantically searched for anything that could be helpful: a *D's Doughnuts* hoodie and hat, a dozen doughnuts and a set of keys. He raced out to find D's old, brown, rusted truck. The key fit the ignition; *churrr*; it didn't start. He tried again. This time she purred like a kitten getting their chin rubbed. He adjusted the mirrors and pulled off the property just in time to pass the fire trucks headed in D's direction.

Chapter 39

Leo drove the surprisingly smooth ride to the closest highway, according to his phone. He kept that—and the jump drive—super close to him. Before entering the highway, he peeled off to what a green sign told him was the last rest stop for the next fifty miles.

Only a handful of cars filled up the parking lot. It housed nothing fancy: a bathroom, a coffee shop (it was closed), and a mini-mart. Large televisions flashed the latest news across the screen, informing drivers of road closures and up-to-the-minute breaking news. It just so happened, *Autumn Log has been captured*, scrolled across the bottom of the screen. The reporter was in Washington D.C. outside of the White House. The anchor sent it over to another reporter at the border, just outside the New North, covering the raiding of Central Park. It appeared military presence was used to sweep the park to prevent people from regrowing trees.

Leo raced to the one-person bathroom. The mirror revealed what he had been too busy to notice: dirt-covered skin, bloodstains, and someone he barely recognized anymore. Tear stains cut through the dirt on his face like a river. His hands were basically lacerated. Closed eyes and deep breaths were his best attempt at steadying his mind. He turned the hot and cold knobs the same amounts, creating a warm stream of water pouring from the faucet, into his hands, washing them clean; he splashed his face. His mind was on a hike. His family's whereabouts were unknown; the girl he was falling in love with was captured, probably in the most secure location in the country.

Knock, knock!

"Almost done," Leo instinctively replied. He got himself together, and when he exited, he smiled and nodded at a younger kid who traded places with him.

Leo headed back to the truck to mull over his plan of attack. The same kid that went into the restroom after Leo was making their way back to their family's minivan. They caught Leo's attention because they stopped walking, started again, and then finally approached. "Here you go, sir," they handed Leo some cash.

He awkwardly reached out and accepted. "Thanks so much. What's your name?"

"I hope it can help you. My name is R.W. Tea II."

"That's a great name! I'm going to vote for you when you run for president," that made them smile. "Can I ask you why you gave me this money?"

"My parents say it's nice to help people we don't even know, especially if we know they are in need," they turned and scampered for their minivan.

Leo shrugged his shoulders. Even though D kept gallons of gas in jerricans in the bed of the truck, he still needed the cash. It was that last phrase the kid said that resonated with him. As he looked at the map, he had a decision to make: New York or D.C.? R.W. Tea II revealed the right thing to do. Leo was headed to D.C. to continue to fight the good fight.

He perused the information on the jump drive. His mind—as messy as his bedroom—was still able to concoct a diabolical-slap-in-the-face plan. There were two trees on the White House grounds, figuring that's where Autumn was being held. According to the intel, President Jamen's desk inside the Oval Office, and the Cabinet Office's meeting table, were assembled from the two trees. It would be a herculean task, but if he was going to rescue Autumn anyway, why not?

Chapter 40

Leo vroomed down various N.U.S. highways, careful not to exceed the legal speed limit: eighty-five miles per hour. His caution required others to peel around him; that, coupled with D's old-school ride, made him stick out of the fancy city like a sore thumb. The closer he got to the downtown area, lights illuminating monuments and memorials lit up the dark sky. There were also billboards at every exit that changed pictures every two seconds. One was an ad for *Now1445* that popped up with Sun's Ray, the hottest singer at the time, promoting his new album. Another was for the latest alcoholic drink. A third was a picture of Autumn. Leo swerved, nearly causing a pileup. Autumn was tied to a chair, with someone's hand forcing her face toward the camera. It was her capture announcement.

Leo veered off the next exit, *Constitution Avenue*, and he slammed the wheel in frustration. "How can this be second nature to people?" he argued with himself. He struggled to connect the dots: how could the government advertise alcohol—something proven to be harmful to people, yet praise the capture of a teenager trying to help the environment? His priorities seemed to be playing a different sport—in a different league—than the masses. The masses were the ones that allowed this to happen... falling right in line with the ways of the past, too scared to inspire a new path which was so incredibly, undeniably the right thing to do.

People looked like ants as Leo cruised by the popular

attractions of the National Mall. He finally found a parking space outside the Jefferson Memorial. One thing that was easily noticeable about Washington D.C. was the droves of people in the streets at all times. There were school trips taking up sidewalks, construction workers building the newest monument, and people jogging—either alone or with a pet. Without Leo's picture flashing all over the billboards, he felt maintaining a low profile was attainable.

On his way up Jefferson's marble steps, a father and son were on the way down.

"No! I want to go to the hotel swimming pool," the son chucked his bag of souvenirs onto the ground.

"I guess the little guy is tired of exploring, huh," Leo picked up the souvenirs from the ground.

The father lifted his child and walked in the opposite direction, abandoning the D.C. gear. Leo picked up the belongings and set them inside the dome, next to one of the twenty-six columns. One item in particular caught his attention: a telescope. It said *Thomas Jefferson's Scope*. It was a burnt-reddish brown color and extended into a foot-long telescope. He tested it out but was soon interrupted.

"Excuse me, young man; is there any way you could please take a picture of us?" an older gentleman extended his phone.

"Sure thing," Leo was happy to accommodate. He snapped the photo of the partners.

One of them inquired about the telescope, "That's a nice one. It's said that Thomas's statue is nineteen feet tall… just tall enough to be able to keep an eye on those in the White House. I bet you could see the White House from here with that telescope…" they walked away, analyzing the photo Leo snapped.

Leo studied Jefferson closer. He walked to the edge of the memorial and jumped up on the highest step. Across the Tidal Basin, he *could* see the White House in the distance. He extended the telescope. After adjusting and focusing, he finally locked in on it. He scanned every window, looking for the smallest morsel of a clue. It seemed all the window treatments were closed, doing their job of securing privacy.

There were signs posted on the South Lawn that read: *Garden Tours*. Tons of kids were walking toward the lawn. He put his thinking cap on. He peeked through the telescope again. A drape flopped around a bit. He focused on it and watched it for a minute. It moved again. Someone else with binoculars was looking out the window; that person gazed out for a solid minute before closing the drape. Leo got the glimpse he needed. He noticed someone with the same color hair as Autumn, chin to chest, seated in a chair. That's really all he could make out. Well, that and the unique color of the walls: blue.

Chapter 41

Leo made his way back to D's truck. He spent the rest of the afternoon familiarizing himself with the D.C. area. High-rise apartment complexes, restaurants and businesses made up the majority of the real estate. Hotels were sprinkled along the corners of most blocks. Streets were populated with seemingly happy people. Musicians and street performers kept folks entertained.

Leo made his way off the touristy-beaten path. He eventually ventured across Ohio Drive, which brought on a flood of emotions; nonetheless, the road led to the Washington Harbor. The White House was no longer in view, but digital signs informed him it was only two miles away. The digital signs lined the entire brown, battered boardwalk; they displayed facts about the area as well as shared live news. He must've looked like a fish out of water; he was the only one reading the information. This spot seemed reserved more for the locals. Regardless, he was learning pertinent information for a potential escape route, so he didn't care how he looked to others. Leo learned from the signs that the Washington Harbor gained access to the Potomac River; the Potomac River led to the Chesapeake Bay, which poured into the Atlantic Ocean. A legion of boats was docked, lined up, and offered tours. If Leo could somehow rescue Autumn, this could serve as their escape route. After all, Autumn snuck into the N.U.S. in a similar fashion.

Leo was lured further down the boardwalk by wafts of

seafood. The further he walked, the less busy it became. The air began to smell like its truer form: dirty sand and trash. An old, tilted sign, barely hanging to a post advertised: *Boat Tours - 1 hour, $200.00 per person.*

He noticed it was the cheapest of any of the tours. No authority officers appeared to be in sight. The boat was small, silver along the sides, and red paint outlined the edges. *Butchie's Boat* was painted on the rear end.

"Interested in a sail?" a larger man practically hollered.

"Just browsing, sir."

"From the looks of it, I'd guess you were debating taking a boat cruise with my ol' girl there," the man used his thumb and pointer finger to remove the lip buildup that made a home in his thick, black goatee.

"Butchie?" Leo proclaimed.

"An honor, Mr...."

"Um... Deal."

"Deal?" Butchie had been around the block a few times. He appeared to be in his fifties and he kept his car's spare tire in his stomach. He went with the flow. "Well, Mr. Deal, why don't we call it an even *whatever you got* for a night cruise for two?" he lifted his eyebrows.

Leo, socially awkward as ever, stumbled, "Who? Um, *us*?"

"Secret's safe with me," he winked. "I've seen your picture around here all week. They just took it off all these screens designed to tell me what to think."

"I'm not sure what you're talking—" Leo tried to deny.

"You can't BS a BS'er, son," Butchie interrupted. He was a rebel, to say the least. His old Harley was in mint condition, kept chained to his boat, and the license plate read: *NVRGTME*. Noticing Leo trying to piece the puzzle together, he helped,

"They'll never get me, son. They tried to get me to ship out of that crowded port," he nodded toward the busier end of the boardwalk. "I told them I only sail for enjoyment. I've fought these dirtbags for years. They still check my boat every time I sail, but most think ol' Butchie is harmless. They won't suspect anything. What time will you and your lady be on the boat?"

Leo's mouth was open like an oyster. "Wow. I don't know what to say," he forked over all his cash from R.W. Tea II.

"Hold tight. There she is right there," Butchie nodded to the digital screens.

Leo went to it like a moth to light. *She's Been Captured* was the headline. It was a livestream. Someone in a mask fumbled the camera to someone else and then started speaking.

Breaking News: President Jamen's Special Message

"Great people of the New United States. We have *had* a federal fugitive on the loose. No more! Your vigilantism has helped lead to her arrest." The camera panned toward Autumn. Her wrists were tied to the arms of a fancy chair that had blue upholstery. It confirmed Leo's hunch as he had caught a glimpse of what he thought was her via telescope earlier that day. The dictator, disguised as the president, continued, "Autumn, welcome to D.C. Fabulous, isn't it?" he smiled and flung his arms in the air. "This is my special friend." The camera found its focus on a masked person who was silently and closely examining a sharp knife. President Jamen jabbered, "It turns out her boyfriend, Leo Oliver, is no longer on her side. He realized their intentions were selfish and silly, so he struck a deal. Do not worry; he will pay, but right now the focus must be on Autumn Log and anyone else *pondering* whether or not they should partake in these *heinous*, *senseless* crimes." His serious attitude and ability to lie would have earned him an Academy Award.

"Ahhh!" Autumn howled in pain as the masked man shoved the knife into her thigh.

"You see, those who provided aid in any way, shape or form, to Autumn or regrowing efforts in general, have been sentenced to life in prison. Plus, as your astute leader, I have done something no other president has done in quite some time: reopened discussion with the New North. Now, they're a bit harsher than me..." President Jamen shook his head, "I mean, us. It turns out they began beating—or even worse—those involved with regrowing trees in Central Park." President Jamen shot a look of *disgust* as a mixture of blood and tears silently evacuated Autumn's body.

"We're only helping—" Autumn was cut off thanks to a slap across the face from President Jamen.

He leaned down on the knife, smiled and claimed, "This is what happens, kids. When you do something you *shouldn't*, you get *punished*. I will not let anyone harm our country. Certainly, I will not let any *trees* be regrown in D.C."

Autumn maintained eye contact with the camera; she refused to shout out in pain a second time.

"Cut!" President Jamen perfectly executed the special announcement, landing jabs in all the right places.

The livestream ended; the digital signs resumed their normal programming.

"Hey, I'm really sorry," Butchie could tell Leo was distraught. He tried to change the subject, "Look, I agree with you kids. I see the changes negatively impacting our waters. It's downright ignorant to know better and not do better. Oh, and I'll be damned if I live in a country that treats anyone, let alone teenagers, like this. And have the *audacity* to put it on live TV?" Butchie huff and puffed and shook his head in disbelief.

Leo might as well have been in a movie; he heard nothing, only mumbles. Frustration defeated his anxieties. His identity finally cemented its home, outbidding anxiety, stress and inaction. He was a person of his word, showed up for others, and did the right thing. He was going to try to rescue Autumn, no matter the cost.

He finally came back, "When's the latest I could catch a ride?"

"Listen, son. I live on this boat. I'll brew my coffee now."

Leo nodded in appreciation.

Chapter 42

"Okay, let's get that knife out of her leg," President Jamen's looks of disgust were still painted all over his face. "We need to keep her alive long enough for the execution," he smirked as he finished the word *execution*.

Autumn spit blood, from the slap she endured, in President Jamen's direction. "What are you talking about?"

"Well, to show the country we captured one of the most wanted fugitives of all time, I thought a public execution would be a nice celebration for the nation's hardships. What do you think?"

"I think you're *psychotic*," she fumed.

He considered her statement. "I only need approval from a few federal judges to make sure it's not an unconstitutional action," President Jamen stood up to straighten his suit and tie. "Shouldn't be, seeing the damages you caused," he winked at her on his way out the door.

"That and the fact you're the reason they're on the bench to begin with," an employee—who was glued to their phone, uttered, and followed President Jamen like a fly on poop.

Two guards remained in the room with Autumn, as had been the case since her arrival. They ushered in a doctor to tend to the gash in her leg. The doctor did a pretty nice job cleaning it up before offering a rather modest recommendation: "She'll need more than slices of bread and water to fully recover." The doctor finished wrapping the wound.

One guard responded, "Not sure that's the intention."

The other guard mocked, "Why waste resources, eh, Autumn?"

The doctor waved their hand in disbelief and exited.

"Doesn't look like she's going anywhere. Let's go see what the rest of the babysitters are up to," one guard led the other out, figuring President Jamen wouldn't be back anytime soon.

Autumn, all alone, deeply exhaled. She took a moment to gather her thoughts and shed some tears, but was right back to working on freeing her wrists from the ropes used to bind them to the chair. She swiveled her butt back and forth on the sturdy, meticulously crafted, fancy chair, hoping to loosen some of its assembly.

As she gathered her surroundings, she noticed everything in the room was blue: the couches, chairs, fancy old décor... you name it. Bumptious chandeliers, seemingly curmudgeon portraits, and obscure foreign objects that looked like weapons, all helped create the unintentional, diabolical environment that was indeed the Blue Room.

The blue window treatments were left peered open the most minuscule amount; the guards usually kept them closed to avoid any unwanted attention drawn Autumn's way. To her delight, she used the surroundings she noticed as an advantage. Through the windows, she saw the Washington Monument. It was gigantic. It looked like it was over five hundred feet tall. If she were able to stand, she would've been able to see the Jefferson Memorial—where Leo discovered hope through a telescope. Autumn needed any and all information as to her whereabouts in foreign territory, especially if she were to break free, which was the goal. She also kept faith burning that Leo wasn't a lost cause, that him leaving her in Groveland wasn't him giving up on her or the mission.

Chapter 43

Leo wandered the National Mall, attempting to inch closer to the White House, blending in as best he could. There were so many school field trips taking place; he saw this as an opportunity to inconspicuously move amongst the masses. Visions of what could have been played pinball in his mind; Maplewood High School took an annual field trip to D.C.—as did every school district in the N.U.S. at some point—when students were seniors. He had it all planned out: he and Cole would be partners, on the same bus as Sierra and Savannah (also partners), and led by their fearless chaperone, Mr. Holt. The trips looked like a blast, especially getting to see them firsthand. Some schools behaved respectfully; other schools let their students run around like wild banshees. The mix worked in Leo's favor, as authority officers in the area had plenty of other people to monitor and occupy their attention.

He walked by a large group of students purchasing souvenirs from street vendors just across from the White House.

"Excuse me," a cheery student tapped Leo's shoulder. "Could you please take a picture of us?" She handed him her cell phone before he answered.

"Sure," he smiled. "Say cheese!" Leo's age difference really showed; the girls' unplanned identical eye rolls at that comment let him know they were most likely in middle school. "Or not!" He sarcastically snarled for his amusement. Instead of saying *cheese*, each person in the photo puckered their lips and held up two fingers.

"Thanks!" One managed as they ran off, contributing to the chaos of two hundred fifty middle schoolers simultaneously purchasing souvenirs.

Leo was learning to take advantage of opportunities. He slid his guilt under the rug and swiped an overpriced green Washington D.C. sweatshirt with ease. Vendors were too busy heckling with preteens; he added to his camouflage.

He slipped on the hoodie, tucked his tarp into his pants a bit better and hopped on the caboose of a group of high school students passing by. They were a respectful group, walking on the right-hand side of the sidewalk—single file, following a chaperone headed straight for the South Lawn of the White House. As they got closer, signs read: *Garden Tours.* The line of students weaved through a mini maze of dirty, silver, iron barricades before entering the South Lawn of the White House. Leo kept moving in rhythm with them.

"Take one! Pass it back!" The chaperone handed back the passes needed in order to enter.

When the passes made their way back to Leo, the stack still had a few flimsy slices remaining. A student handed it to him without paying attention, and Leo accepted the stack and kept the pass-it-back idea moving, handing it to a chaperone from another school, whose class was now directly behind him. Their chaperone leading that group declined the passes, noting they had their own. Leo nodded and pocketed the extra passes. He was closing in on Autumn quicker than he anticipated.

Chapter 44

There Leo was: sandwiched between two class trips and not raising any red flags. Eventually, the groups' journey through the gardens came to a fork in the tour. One path said *Entrance 1* and the other *Entrance 2*. Leo's "original" class, in which he was the caboose, aimed for *Entrance 1*, and the other class he was in front of, *Entrance 2*. He looked at the ticket: *Garden Tour and White House Tour*. This was literally his ticket inside. It appeared many schools took advantage of this opportunity, as the line to get inside the residency was quite long.

After fifteen minutes or so, the group was led along a red carpet, taking baby steps because they were packed in like sardines, to the White House Lobby.

When they finally made their way inside the lobby, a person leading the tour projected through a megaphone, "Okay, looks like that is everybody for this tour slot. My name is Misty and wel—" she was interrupted.

"Welcome!" President Jamen surprisingly shouted from atop the staircase in the center of the lobby, riding high from his special announcement. "Mi casa, su casa. Ah," he took a deep breath and looked around, "the youth sure is looking bright. Enjoy your tour. Misty, please give this fine group of young patriots the special tour," he walked away as students stared up, unable to close their mouths.

"Wow, what a treat!" Misty, who was *very peppy*, shouted through the megaphone, unaffected by the painful roaring that rattled everyone else's eardrums. "Most groups never hear from President Jamen. I think he's pretty happy having captured that criminal and all. President Jamen is just passing through from his office—*which is off-limits*, to the Blue Room—which is *usually* part of the tour, but off-limits today," she smiled, unaware that she revealed the location of the teenage prisoner.

A student raised their hand; Misty called on them. "Why is it off-limits?"

"Never mind that, my dear. Instead, we'll replace it with some special treats. Now, now... right this way," the tour commenced.

Leo now knew the direction of both his intended destinations: the Blue Room to rescue Autumn, and the President's Oval Office where he'd find the materials to regrow two trees.

Misty did do a *dynamite* job, leading them to the kitchen, lounge areas, select workrooms and the private movie theater. It would have been a pretty sweet experience and setup had the president not been a mind controlling, propaganda spreading, psychopathic dictator.

In fact, as the tour progressed, that personality slowly started to come to life in the residency's design. The floors were plain, old, and the black and white tiles were in desperate need of an update. Most of the furniture and woodwork had a dark stain. Although undeniably beautiful, everything was a bit bland, basic and clearly for show.

A student from another group raised their hand. "Where are the rooms for kids?"

"There are currently no children living in the White House," Misty answered with a grin.

"Is that why it looks so boring? And dark?" another student asked. Their chaperone's eyes widened in disbelief.

A few workers looked through the top end of their bifocals, momentarily straying from the papers they were so intently examining.

Misty giggled a little and ignored the question, "Okay, let's move along now, shall we? We are going to end the tour with a quick peek inside the Presidential Garage. Notice there are five black SUVs," she glided her hands as if hosting a game show. "Each time the president leaves the grounds, four of these five vehicles hit the streets. That way, nobody is ever really sure the president's exact location as they motorcade through the capital. The SUVs have tinted windows, are bulletproof and ensure protection of all those inside."

Everyone had an opportunity to file into the garage and see the different vehicles.

It wasn't long until: *Wee woo! We woo! We woo!* Someone touched one of the large pieces of steel. Misty opened a cabinet drawer, grabbed a set of keys and pushed the red alarm button to end the overtly loud warning signal.

In the midst of the mess, one student dropped their cell phone on the ground. The flash from the camera snapped. Misty was thrown off; she stomped her feet rapidly in fear. Pockets of laughter filled the air.

Leo saw this as another opportunity. He bent down to tie his shoe but secretly slipped underneath one of the SUVs. His heart pounded like a drum.

"Okay, enough!" Misty was not as amused as the others. "This tour has concluded! The sheer rudeness will most likely get your school banned from ever stepping foot on the White House grounds again!" The students were shuffled back inside to put the final touches on the *interesting* excursion.

Slam! The door shut. Leo finally exhaled. He was alone in the Presidential Garage, lying atop the gray, cool, cement floor.

Chapter 45

Leo crawled out from underneath the SUV. He headed toward the key drawer Misty utilized earlier. On his way over, he stumbled over something. It was a drain plate, and it nearly tripped him. He bent down to take a closer look; it sounded like a stream of water was flowing underground. He slipped his fingers into the red, rusted plate, and pulled it up and off to the side. Water flowed in a seemingly shallow collection of water. It was too interesting *not* to investigate. The shute leading down had a thin circumference; he was narrowly able to squeak through. It was a good thing he hadn't been eating much lately.

He carefully lowered himself down on the three-step ladder until he had his footing in the ankle-high water. He made sure to cover the drain plate above… just in case. Leo used his cell phone's flashlight to provide a view—although faint at best. The dark tunnel channeled water with a minor current toward what resembled an abyss. Leo carefully inched through the water.

After a few moments, a single ray of light appeared in the distance. He picked up the pace. The light grew brighter with every step he took. The water and path met at a dead end. The only way to go was up; another three-step ladder provided access to another drain plate. Leo pushed it up and to the side. Out of an abundance of caution, he poked his head up, like a groundhog, to survey the area.

The view showcased the opposite end of the White House: the North Lawn. Leo snuck his head out further, like a turtle from its shell, making sure the coast was clear. It was *not* clear. Authority officers were scattered about the roof of the White House, all with weapons strapped across their chests. Luckily, the streets were consumed with a plethora of people drawing their attention: school trips, tourists, the homeless, protesters… they all blended together.

Leo couldn't help but notice how green the grass was. Sprinklers sprayed water in all directions, in a delayed-type fashion. That, coupled with a mammoth-sized fountain in the center of the North Lawn, was most likely the reason for the drain. The fountain spouted water into the air. It was the perfect opportunity to pose for a picture, as many school students did. It appeared, from a distance, they tried to trick the camera to make it look like they were either drinking the water or taking a pee. Teenagers.

Leo looked a little closer; two slices of grass appeared to be a much different shade of green. It looked like fake grass, perhaps turf. He checked the materials list again; the two trees he wanted to regrow were on the North Lawn. He figured the stumps were probably being covered by the turf.

The material list showed the trees were used for the president's personal desk and the Cabinet's meeting table—which served as the meeting spot for President Jamen's trusted advisors. The trees themselves told an interesting story. The dwarf chestnut oak tree had a special note next to the material list…

Note: Gift from Canada.

It came rushing back to him; his history teacher, Mr. Ferris, showed his class video clips of President Jamen announcing the changes in the relationship between the two countries, suggesting they were no longer allies. Canada didn't take it too kindly when

President Jamen made a spectacle of him chopping it down for his personal desk. The tree was a gift from Canada to symbolize strength and regrowth following the attacks that split up the former United States, roughly eighty years ago.

"To symbolize our independence from any past we have ever been a part of," were President Jamen's exact words, which Mr. Ferris was required by law to make students memorize. The desk's design—so intricate—required all the wood from the tree; regrowing this one was feasible, if not a walk in the park compared to what they accomplished at Groveland.

The other tree, also a gift from a former ally, during a former administration, was used to assemble the president's Cabinet meeting table. Leo assumed this tree would be a little bigger and more challenging of a task. Although, who knows just how large the dictator disguised as a president's Cabinet could be? Regardless, the material list was one item: simple enough. The tree itself was labeled a Cedrus libani. All it said in the notes is that it was a gift from peace efforts in the Middle East. Leo was at least happy his country was able to work with others at one point in its history; it was hard to imagine given its current standing.

He got what he needed. Now he had to find Autumn.

Chapter 46

Meanwhile, President Jamen and his group of goons finished their lunch in the Blue Room, taunting Autumn with delicious delicacies and aromas. "What to do, what to do, what to do?" President Jamen ticked his tongue and batted the corners of his mouth with a napkin, analyzing her.

"Could let me go," Autumn suggested, wasting her breath. "Not sure why you like hanging out with me so much," she insinuated their lunches, which had become regular over the past few days, had run their "charming" course already.

President Jamen laughed uncontrollably. "Listen here, sweetie—"

"Do *not* sweetie me," Autumn was taught to never let a person belittle another, especially with terms of endearment, and even more, not an old man to a young woman.

"I'll tell you what, you sure are likeable," President Jamen caked on the sarcasm thicker than frosting on a toddler's birthday cake. "It's no wonder your lover boy wised up."

"What do you mean?" Autumn eventually took the bait.

"I told you about his offer," President Jamen reminded.

"So," Autumn didn't see the point.

"The point is, he stopped regrowing trees. He has everything necessary to do so, including the material lists and capable contacts."

"Debatable," Autumn protested. "You've locked up Phoenix, Toll and Alder. You've isolated—if not worse—Leo from his family. Not sure he has *anyone*."

"*Poor baby*!" President Jamen sarcastically moaned.

"You're an emotionally immature adult." Bullseye; Autumn struck a nerve, as everyone in the room paused and looked at her.

"What did you say?" President Jamen asked even though he clearly heard.

"Excuse me, Mr. President. It is imperative you see this," one of his cronies extended a message they received on their phone, unintentionally de-escalating the situation.

"What? Another catastrophe?" Autumn tried to distract him as he read. "How many have died, *this time*, as a result of extreme, unpredictable weather or natural disasters due to your inaction? Is it your oil fields' fault? Too much drilling making people in the surrounding communities sick?" Autumn knew he wanted her alive for the public-celebration-execution thingy, so she found the confidence to let her feelings fly with no filter.

President Jamen peered and took a deep breath. He chucked the phone across the room with no regard for personal property. He even broke what appeared to be a very expensive vase in the process. "Let's go!"

Whatever consumed his rage was Autumn's friend for the moment.

Chapter 47

Leo scaled his way back to the garage. He was on the top step of the three-step ladder when he heard:
Slam!
Slam!
Two car doors slammed shut.
"What is *he* doing in D.C.? I'm going to *kill* his family!" President Jamen howled.
"There was an anonymous tip reported. It seems Leo was spotted near Arlington National Cemetery, up by the Arlington House."
Slam!
Slam!
Two more car doors shut and the warmth of the engines poured fumes down the drain. Leo struggled to hold in his cough—best he could—until he heard the large garage door open, the SUVs wheel out, and the large garage door close.
Cough! Cough! He shooed the exhaust away from his air space. He wiggled up through the tight squeeze of the drain plate opening, walked over to the key drawer and pocketed the keys to the SUV that was left behind. He had no idea who reported him at Arlington. The only thing he thought was that some handsome looking kid got mistaken for him at the Arlington House.
He played the role of a secret agent, inching open the side door and slowly surveying the room before stepping foot back inside the White House. He didn't notice many authority officers

on the tour; he retraced the route as best he could. He worked his way past the fancy workrooms and movie theater and eventually closed in on where the tours began. He knew—because of President Jamen's cocky behavior, he'd have to cross the large staircase to the other end of the White House. He waited. And waited, like a vigilant pedestrian at a crosswalk. And when the next tour began, he snuck across, blending in with the flow, beautifully. The tour went one way, and he, another.

He came across the kitchen; a sign caught his attention, deeper within the kitchen, causing him to do a double take. It read: *Chocolate Shop*. That caught his attention quicker than green grass through a goose.

"Yo! I'll be right back! Have to go to the other chocolate shop, if you catch my drift," a younger employee unwittingly helped Leo; they removed their pastry chef jacket and headed out of the kitchen. "Can't believe there's no designated bathrooms for us."

Leo closed his eyes and took a deep breath, hoping to generate confidence. Remembering the importance of *action*, he stepped into the kitchen. Work in the kitchen and *Chocolate Shop* was clockwork. People had a plan, moved in formations and paid no mind to anything standing in the way of their short-term goals.

Leo snuck in and removed the pastry chef jacket off the coat rack that was holding it up and slid it over his D.C. hoodie. He had his camouflage… again. He grabbed a tray, which of course had chocolates on it, and went back along his route, now hustling in the direction of the Blue Room.

He passed people, smiling and nodding when unintentional eye contact was created. He passed more closed doors with every step down the hall. He finally made it to the last room he could enter, on his left. The plaque on the door confirmed he made it to the *Blue Room*.

He cocked the golden, oblong door handle down and gently pushed the door in. He did it: he found Autumn, still tied to the chair.

Chapter 48

"Fancy meeting you here," he smiled at her after noticing they had the room to themselves.

Autumn was in disbelief. "What? Are you kidding me? Where? How?" She puttered like a car trying to start.

"Yes, I usually make the ladies lose their minds," he joked, taking the wrist restraints off her. "I brought you some chocolate," he handed her a piece that was on the tray. "We have to go."

They were on their way out when they heard footsteps outside the door. "Wait! The guards are back," Autumn slumped back in her chair.

Leo grabbed his tray and walked toward the door. It swung open. The two guards stood still. "What are you doing in here, chocolate boy?" they mocked in a demeaning tone.

"I was told to deliver this chocolate delicacy to President Jamen. I heard he might be in here," Leo presented the tray as if he were a veteran server.

"He's not here. We'll take them though," one guard stuffed the chocolates in his pocket. "You can leave now, chocolate boy."

"Chocolate boy," Leo maliciously snickered. "I love it! Have a great day!" He wound up and smacked a guard with the tray. The guard fell to the blue and white rug, sprinkling it with red, thanks to blood oozing from the tray's impact.

The other guard punched Leo and knocked him to the

ground. He drew his weapon, pointing it at Leo. "Don't move!"

Autumn silently sprang into action, grabbed one of the obscure foreign objects off the wall and swung it across the guard's back. *Swoosh!* She dropped him faster than Leo went down.

"Brings back memories," Leo picked himself up. "I felt the breeze, slugger. I did that to you and you *still* talk to me?" They tied the guards to the chairs with duct tape and stuffed their mouths with old rags that were used on Autumn. "Here, put this on," Leo tossed her the D.C. hoodie. "If we get caught, tell them you were on a tour and got lost. Follow me."

Autumn followed Leo beyond the hallway of closed doors, back to where the tours commenced. As they walked down the hall, Leo urged, "The president is out right now. I have a plan. Trust me." Autumn nodded, signaling her consent.

Once Misty departed with the next tour, they coolly walked up the long staircase. As they made small talk to avoid seeming out of place, Leo pretended to point out things, making it look like he was training her to become better acclimated with serving or something; perhaps it looked like he was giving her an extended tour of sorts. Whatever it was, they blended into the never-ending commotion of the working folks in the White House.

They reached the top of the steps and took a right, following signs pointing toward the Oval Office. Their incognito act worked. They passed people who were either preoccupied with phone calls or that simply didn't ask questions. Leo, acting like it was indeed his job, extended his hand to meet the cool, golden, circular doorknob. He pushed the door open, "Chocolate delivery," and closed it behind them. They were alone in the president's personal office.

Time was short and nerves were high, but that didn't stop Leo from setting down the tray and pulling Autumn close to him; the two shared a passionate kiss before snapping back to reality.

"I'm so sorry I left you in that jail. I didn't have a choice," Leo felt Autumn's face and examined her body, hoping not to find anything too severely wrong.

"I figured," Autumn went in for another kiss, erasing the unsettling feelings she'd been wrestling with of never seeing him again.

"I have the materials list," Leo led Autumn to the window, which oversaw the North Lawn. "There are two tree stumps there," Leo pointed to what he discovered through the drain system. "One is for *this* desk," they examined the craftily designed hunk of wood. It was superfluous and engraved with a bald eagle—a symbol of freedom, which seemed ironic to them. The excessive engravings had the words: power, strength and justice, etched for all to read.

"Just this desk?" Autumn was also shocked by the apparent ease of regrowing this tree.

"Just this desk," Leo doubled down. "The second tree is for the Cabinet's meeting table. It's directly across the hall."

"Just the table?" Autumn's disbelief transformed into excitement.

"Just the table," Leo's palms pointed to the air, unsure how else to convey his pleasure.

"Okay. Let's do it!" Autumn was all in.

"We can do this! I have the keys to our getaway car," he dangled them as proof. "Once we have the desk and table by the window, I'll go pull around front."

"It's a long shot," Autumn stated obvious. "But I guess they were going to execute me anyway."

"They're not doing that today," Leo led the way across the hall to the Cabinet Room. It was vacant as well. His inner circle must've really been in a rush to get to the Arlington House. Leo and Autumn propped the doors open and tag teamed maneuvering the table into the Oval Office.

"Can I help you two?" a passerby halted their transplant.

"Just doing our job," Leo was becoming a natural at lying. "President Jamen has requested a spread of the nation's finest chocolates waiting for his Cabinet at their next meeting. Training this one today," Leo nodded at Autumn. "When the president wants something, he gets it," he smiled, acting like he was teaching Autumn.

"You two are good kids for obeying. We *also* have learned not to question *his* greatness," the passerby encouraged them before continuing with their personal endeavors.

Leo and Autumn locked eyes, knowing they narrowly escaped. They closed the doors to the Oval Office and scootched the desk and table next to the window. They unlocked it and extended the heavy, most likely bulletproof, window open.

"When you see me pull around, pop out the screen and push them down. The windows open far enough for them to slide right on through. Try to float them on top of the SUV; they're indestructible. I can drive them to the stumps. We'll regrow and book it out of here."

"They're going to catch us. We can't just drive out of town."

Leo filled her in about Butchie's boat and the plan to escape by water. "We can do this." He grabbed her hand and kissed it before exiting with his tray.

Chapter 49

Autumn wasn't comfortable. She walked over to the door and locked it. She didn't have a chef's jacket she could hide behind.

Meanwhile, Leo played his cards so he crossed paths with Mindy's tour group as they left the Presidential Garage. To his avail, the president wasn't back yet.

Leo unlocked the SUV, pushed the button to start it and programmed the vehicle's GPS to the marina. He scanned the overhead visor; he clicked the garage door opener. It felt like an eternity, but it finally became fully ajar. He gently pulled out and around the driveway. The North Lawn was in view; he slowly pounced over some shrubs.

He kept looking up, maneuvering the SUV as close to the Oval Office as possible. He saw Autumn waving from the window: bingo. He backed up, hoping the table and desk could just float directly onto the SUV's roof.

He peered up again; snipers on the rooftop and other authority officers began their panic. They were scrambling, clearly active on their walkie-talkies.

Bang!

"What the!" Leo screamed. It was the president's desk. Autumn popped out the window screen and sent the desk tumbling onto the top of the car.

Bang! The Cabinet's meeting table towered on top.

Bang! Autumn wasted no time. She jumped out of the Oval Office window, onto the roof of the SUV; Leo let her in on the passenger side.

"I wasn't ready!"

"Too bad! Drive!" Autumn hollered. "Someone spotted me, and they were trying to break into the Oval Office. They know something is wrong. I smashed a man's hand in the door!" Blood started to evacuate her wrapped leg. "They're coming for us!"

Bullets confirmed that. *Pew! Pew! Pew!* Bullets rained down on the black SUV; thankfully Misty was right: they did no harm to the heavy piece of military-grade steel. Leo trenched toward the stumps, and parked the SUV so it served as a shield between the snipers' bullets and the stumps.

They both hopped out of the passenger-side door. Spectators were snapping pictures and recording video of the debacle. Whispers became yells as the streets grew with discontent. Authority vehicle sirens filled the air. *Wee woo!*

"They're going to shoot someone!" Leo screamed, signaling for the pedestrians to get out of the way.

They were running out of time; they reached on top of the roof and pulled the Cabinet meeting table down.

Pew! Snipers were locked in; their precise aim narrowly missed their phalanges.

They did the same thing with President Jamen's personal desk. After some pushing and shoving, both stumps had the materials set, as each stump was on the furthest end of the SUV.

Authority officers rapidly scampered, better angling themselves for a clearer shot.

Leo removed the tarp he had hidden inside the lining of his pants. He started with the president's desk.

"Get in and drive forward. This tree is going to be huge!" Leo demanded, knowing Autumn couldn't easily move. If the tree destroyed their cover, they'd shoot her. "We can do this!

Three! Two! One!" he yanked the tarp away.

Pew! Leo's head went down like a whack-a-mole.

Luckily, the gift from Canada darted into the air, confusing onlookers. The dwarf chestnut oak stood over fifteen feet tall, dangling acorns off the leaves: something new to Leo and Autumn.

Pew! Pew! Pew! It was apparent the confusion of a tree regrowing spawned fear. Suddenly, people started to scatter throughout the streets, running in panic. The irony of not running when bullets first sounded, but instead at the rebirth of a tree, showed society's unflattering true colors.

Autumn inched the SUV up ever so slightly. Leo scurried to continue to use the SUV as a shield. The tree benevolently served as protection as well. He tried to cover the Cabinet meeting table; it couldn't all fit under the tarp. "Move up more!"

Autumn did. She caught on to the dilemma. She removed her sweatshirt and tossed it in his direction. Leo removed his chef's jacket. They'd never attempted anything like this before, but it was their only chance.

Authority officers were settling into place; a perimeter outside the North Lawn was being established—most likely at President Jamen's request. The "family-friendly" nation's capital was a war zone; souls sprinted in all directions. Be that as it may, it did not deter the gunfire from those sworn to protect those very same souls.

In the midst of the chaos, Leo took a deep breath and acted. He lofted the tarp over the majority of the table; he was then forced to step outside the SUV's protection to inch the sweatshirt and chef's jacket over the remaining portion of the table. Leo became the target for the snipers' target practice. He gripped a corner of all three pieces covering the table—the tarp, hoodie and chef's jacket—and just as he was about to pull them off... *Pew!* A bullet struck his shoulder. He wailed in agony as he fell to the ground. Fortunately, the force sent him backward, helping remove the coverings.

A Cedrus libani tree magnificently blossomed in, literally, the blink of an eye; the eighty-foot, 3D-looking-layered tree, colored with greenery, provided shelter for Autumn to sneak back out the passenger door to help Leo.

Pew! A bullet grazed her hip; she jumped back for cover. Leo was forced to army crawl to her. They mustered every ounce of strength they had left to scooch back inside the SUV, leaving trails of blood behind in the process. They took turns helping one another until Leo was in the driver seat, quickly turning the steering wheel to head back toward the South Lawn; the North Lawn not only had a strong perimeter established, but it had too many innocent people in the vicinity.

To their shock, very few bullets were fired at the SUV. Many secret service snipers and authority officers were too taken aback by the act to fully understand what was going on. Their reality seemed challenged.

"Ahh!" Autumn applied pressure to her hip area; her bullet and stab wounds made the lower part of her body feel a burning numbness.

Leo took off his shirt and tried to apply pressure to his shoulder. He became woozier by the second; too much blood was flowing from the bullet hole. The bumps the SUV endured from off-roading didn't help either; it might as well have had hydraulics.

The voice on the SUV's GPS kept getting cut off due to the high volume of reroutes. Traffic had been suspended and roads were closed off. Leo, making his face—this time due to physical pain—drove out of the National Mall area, across Ohio Drive, and somehow made it to the marina. When they were close enough to Butchie's boat, they evacuated the SUV one last time.

A small flight of old, uneven, cracked steps served as the last obstacle before they reached their getaway. There was traffic on the waters; boats dispersed, trying to catch a glimpse of what was now all over the large display televisions. Traffic on the roads was at a standstill. *Honk*! *Beep*! There was no way they would have made it if it hadn't been for the off-road driving.

The two wobbled down the steps, using each other as crutches. When they finally made it to the boardwalk, they were greeted by their captain.

"Welcome to your dinner cruise," Butchie emphatically proclaimed. He wasted no time in helping the battered couple below deck of his humble vessel. He scattered his mess of papers onto the ground, further contributing to the already existing pigsty. Once his kitchen table was cleared off, he laid Leo back and gave him items to help apply pressure to prevent blood loss. He set up Autumn with a similar spot, on a small leather couch with rips in it. Once he got them laid down, he quickly learned the severity of the situation. Unfortunately, authority sirens hovered nearby, and Butchie had to leave the pair below deck in order to set sail.

"You kids stay alive! I have to launch us out of here."

Chapter 50

Butchie navigated his way down the Potomac toward the Chesapeake Bay. When boat traffic cleared a bit, he rushed down to help Autumn and Leo.

Autumn broke the awkward silence with: "Hey, I'm Autumn."

"Yeah, I know… I'm Butchie. Nice to officially meet you."

Autumn was sitting up; her bleeding was plugged for the moment. "I had some water. I hope that's all right."

"Of course, of course," Butchie gently placed his fingers on Leo's throat. "He still has a pulse."

"I know. He was talking to me but drifted off. I couldn't understand him."

Butchie went to his minifridge to get some more bottles of water. "I served in the military. They put you through hell and teach you all kinds of survival tips, even though we'd never see hand-to-hand combat these days." Butchie poked Leo's arm with a needle. He made a makeshift fluid drip to prevent dehydration. "Are *you* feeling all right?"

"Yeah. Just a little tired and beat up," Autumn felt bad complaining when it was unclear if Leo was going to pull through.

Butchie could sense it. He tried to switch up the topic. "He'll be all right. I thought the phony tip about him being at the Arlington House would create some more time."

"That was you?" Autumn pieced President Jamen's phone

call together—the one back from when she was in that *awful* Blue Room.

"Listen, I'll tend to this bullet hole if you can guide us along these waters," Butchie already started working.

Autumn happily obliged. "I've captained a boat or two in my day, being from Florida and all." On her way up, she stopped to kiss Leo's closed eyes. Butchie showed her the very basic ropes of how to guide the boat, then returned to tend to Leo's needs. Autumn looked out and saw nothing but open water. It was almost too soothing. The breeze and smells of salt invited her to reflect on her journey; in spite of that, she wasn't ready to process anything just yet. The next steps were still so uncertain.

An hour couldn't have passed. "How is he?" Autumn quickly dried her eyes, not expecting Butchie above deck so soon. She kept her eyes fixated on the open water, afraid of the answer.

"We'll see. Bullet's out. Bleedin's stopped. Stitches in. He's got fluids pumping in his arm as well as an antibiotic to kill any germs you kids picked up on your adventure."

"Wow! You stay prepared. Is there anything else we can do?"

"Think positively; life is a mindset," Butchie took over the wheel. "This is for you," he extended the last of his pain medicine. "You'll have to take it easy; when he wakes up, he's going to need your help."

Autumn nodded her head. She swallowed back her fears along with the medicine. "Thank you."

"Thank *you two*."

"For what?" Autumn chuckled, unsure what Butchie could possibly mean.

"Well, for your courage."

Autumn didn't respond.

Butchie continued, "See, like your family, Autumn, I believe that trees are important too. Being out to sea, I've seen the changes over the years; I've had to rebuild my dock many times... darn rising sea levels."

Autumn didn't respond.

Butchie had the gift of gab, "I have been following the news story since you guys regrew around that hospital. Rumor has it you needed one thousand trees. I sail all around the N.U.S. and I've heard through the grapevine you're close."

Autumn smiled. "I *think* we did it. My family is in the S.U.S.; Leo's in the New North. I guess only time will tell. I really don't know."

"I've also heard you're not alone. It seems you've inspired many others to question their government's actions regarding our environment."

"Leo will be happy to hear that when he wakes up."

"That's the optimism I like to hear," Butchie slapped his steering wheel with excitement, playing it like a bongo drum. He broke out into what Autumn could only guess was an old sailor's song turned original.

"Sailin' these deep blue seas,
Fishing for some fishies,
They'll never catch Butchie,
They can kiss my tushie!"

Butchie held the *E* way too long. Autumn used it as her opportunity to limp back below deck.

The team sailed for a few hours. Autumn continued to tend to Leo's wounds as best she could; he was still out like a light. "You know, you are an excellent napper," Autumn babbled all kinds of sweet nothings, taking Butchie's advice of being a chatterbox to help him wake sooner.

Butchie stomped on the floor, indicating something was wrong. Autumn rushed back to the deck. "What's going on?"

"We're getting close to the Atlantic Ocean. Authority officer boats are patrolling the area," Butchie said while scanning through his binoculars. "Have a look." He handed her the binoculars. "We're going to dip into S.U.S. waters. We're going to have to part ways."

"What are you talking about? We're in the middle of the ocean. The sun is setting; it's going to be nothing but us and the stars pretty soon," Autumn tensed.

"We're not far from some coastal towns. I have a plan." Butchie started unwrapping a black plastic raft. He could sense Autumn's concern. "Don't panic; it's military grade and has a motor." He tied it to the side of his boat and let it finish blowing up on top of the water. "Just keep the motor running. If you sail through the night, you're going to be at the southern tip of the S.U.S. Should be plenty of beach towns to run wild in."

"The waves seem too aggressive; it's too small. Are we going to make it?"

"Not sure. The deal was to get you as far as I could. That's here. I know people who have tried this very journey. Don't know if they've made it."

"Leo's not up yet," Autumn was about to be not *up a creek*, but *up an ocean* without a paddle… literally.

"There are boats out yonder. We must be past the border. They're coming after us," Butchie helped lift Leo onto the raft. "You got this. Give it five minutes, then start the motor. Keep heading south," he handed Autumn an old compass he kept around his neck, clearly of sentimental value to him.

"Thank you," Autumn said genuinely, as she was assisted onto the raft. She placed it around her neck. "I'll take good care of this compass. I lost my other one—"

"No problem!" Butchie rushed her along. He helped zip part of the boat up with a cover so it'd be less exposed. "It's sturdier than it looks." He pushed it away from his craft. "Remember, give me five minutes, then you go!" He let the raft drift a bit. "Come get me!" He added a few choice words as he sped off toward the authority boats.

Chapter 51

The night sky got comfortable; the stars were the most beautiful nightlight. It sounded like a baby's sound machine: waves, wind, and somehow silence.

Autumn steered the boat, using one hand to guide it and the other to hold up Leo's head. Waves constantly splashed them. It was a clear night but still, if Autumn had a nickel for every time a wave nearly flipped over the raft, she'd be rich. *Army Issued* is what the tag read on the side. That eased Autumn's nerves—the military used this raft for serious missions. Even though it appeared iffy, it proved reliable so far.

Autumn could no longer fight the bloodshot strain screaming from her eyes. She closed them just as the tip of the yellow sun poked its head out of the horizon. It seemed to happen in unison: her falling asleep and b*oom*!

She woke up flustered. The raft hit something, sending Autumn into the air and splashing into the water. Leo plopped into the ocean. Thankfully, they hit some piece of land. It was the beginning of a beach. Autumn struggled to her feet. She immediately dove back into the waters, unable to locate Leo.

"Leo!" she screamed between plunges, knowing it was no use. She noticed something in the distance. It looked like it could be him. She tried a combination of running and swimming through the waves. It *was* him! He was not moving. Autumn used the help of the tides to power him toward the white sand that made up the shore.

Unsure if he was still breathing, she performed CPR the best she could. She launched 30 chest compressions. Finally, water spouted out of his mouth.

He was still unresponsive; but she saw his chest moving up and down, slowly. She pounded the soft, white sand and cried, laying over his chest. She never thought in a million years she'd be *here*. They'd regrown so many trees and probably saved the planet. Despite all that, it seemed deflating to think they'd only be remembered as notorious criminals. She never thought in a million years that her *helping* would cause so much damage or that she'd *still* be so far away from her family. The plan was to save the world and go back to their normal lives: naivety.

She wrestled with her guilt. She put a young man that she *just* met in danger—a whole family that she just met in danger. She couldn't shake responsibility for Leo's potential outcome. A person she fell in love with might die because of *her*, at least that's how her mind was playing it at the moment. She couldn't believe she fell in love. And now she sat on a beach, wondering if she'd ever be found. Here, in this blip of reality, her mind was better than any prison President Jamen could ever design.

Meanwhile, skinny, broken pieces of driftwood floated ashore. The soft, white-sand beach was home to little crabs, who didn't appreciate their new roommates. Small black specs were noticeable throughout parts of the beach, ingrained in the sand; Autumn lived in the S.U.S. and knew this was due to a lack of population in the area.

She hiked up the gradual incline of this small, inhabitable, little chunk of land. Unfortunately, she could see the entire island. It was indeed abandoned; it was a hundred yards by a hundred yards, maybe. There were no trees; there were a few stumps, but no products to regrow them. There was no apparent reason for any living thing to ever visit this island.

She peered straight through the tall grasses and out to nothing but more open ocean. As she deeply exhaled, something in the distance caught her eye: even further south, she could see what appeared to be a stretch of these similar mini islands.

Khak, khak! A coughing noise broke her train of thought.

Autumn sprinted back down the incline, practically sliding like a snowboarder on the sand. Leo was awake.

"Are you okay?" She hugged him a touch too hard.

Leo nodded his head. "Where are we?" He grimaced as he noticed his stitches for the first time.

"I don't know. Butchie sailed us out of D.C. and gave us a raft. We drifted all night and landed here like an hour ago."

"What happened to Butchie?"

"He distracted the authority boats," Autumn chuckled. "After disguising our raft, he floored it. The top half of his boat was in the air. He went full speed right at them, and I swear I heard him call them every name in the book."

"He's a good man," Leo couldn't help but smile.

"He fixed you up nicely. I think we're off the coast of Florida somewhere. I haven't seen a soul, a sign of land or shade."

Leo checked his phone. "Dead."

"Mine too."

Leo wrestled with his pain and made his way to his feet. They supported each other as they gimped along the beach, searching for anything to help. They noted the need to explore the other mini islands. And while that may have been true, they needed to rest first.

They sluggishly settled down on the sand, toes in the water. Leo splashed Autumn as the waves broke in on them. She couldn't help but be a little happy. "We did it. I *think*. I *think* we saved the planet! We're right around a thousand trees like Rea said. Butchie told me people were growing them all over. That must've been why President Jamen was so angsty about leaving the White House… trying to stop you. We must be close."

"Yeah, we did save and hopefully change the world," Leo was pumped. "People lift people!"

"What? Is that your motivational insight after everything we've been through?"

"It just came to me. I don't know what it means. But I think it makes sense."

Leo leaned in for a long, passionate kiss.

He stared at Autumn for too long. "What?" She didn't like it.

"Nothing."

"Just tell me."

"Well," he started, "I know this isn't ideal, but I think I might be in love with you, Autumn Log."

Autumn let an awkward one Mississippi worth of silence pass by for fun. "I love *you*."

Their lips locking confirmed they were no longer the same kids—the same people—and that was okay.

What wasn't okay, was where they stood, physically. They stood on soggy, sandy, deserted strips of islands. Each island was separated by swimmable distances of gray, choppy Atlantic waters. Each appeared in the distance like miniature mountains with steep uprisings, then went flat; place your hand flat on a table. Move your eyes low, and pretend you're a spec on the table a mere inch away. There was an incline like your thumb, then flat like your hand. Beyond that: a mystery.

The day slowly crept by. The helpless heroes held hands as

suspicious storm clouds jogged into view and darted rain at their heads.

"It's all right! This is the best thing that could happen!" Autumn shouted.

"How so?" Leo probed rather calmly as water began to pour into his mouth. They had no shelter. Lightning struck in the distance.

"We'll be able to see clearly when it passes. Plus, it's better than the sun burning us."

That optimism was cut short by the water vastly accumulating, forcing them to explore the next island sooner than originally intended. The raft was out of gas and wouldn't be helpful for this mission.

Splash!

The pair switched between freestyle, breaststroke, backstroke, butterfly… you name it, just to get to the next island.

The choppy waves were a worthy opponent, especially given their injuries and the storm. They spewed water from their mouths as they finally made their way to the shores. They arrived at the next mini island; it had the same makeup as the first one. To their dismay, it also appeared to be sinking with the added rainwater.

Splash!

Same story for the next island, and each island after that, until they reached the last one in the string of mini islands. The last one was peculiar. It was more mountainous; in order to get proper footing, they had to scale several large rocks upon emerging from the water.

Strange voices and noises tinkered in the background. They made their way up the top of the steep siding. Their eyes became magnets, staring at each other in disbelief. A green sign with white lettering read: *Welcome to Etre Island*!

Printed in the USA
CPSIA information can be obtained
at www.ICGtesting.com
LVHW041525280624
784124LV00025BB/68